Waiting for You

Camden Grove Series: Book 3

Tessa Kinkade

Also By

Tessa Kinkade

Camden Grove Series
The Perfect Shot
Picture This

For Spencer,

Because of your words and a two-year wait, the idea for this book came into being.

Chapter One

Maddox

Maddox Granger rolled into Camden Grove on a Friday afternoon, restlessness swelling in his chest like a slow-rising tide. The unseasonably warm November weather, comfortable enough for him to remove the Jeep's soft top, had done little to settle his doubts. For every mile he traveled closer to the small town, he also drew nearer to openly acknowledging things he knew would change his life—the kind of things that people don't turn away from.

Plenty had shifted in six years. The last he'd seen of Paige Westerfield, they were just kids really and, as it would seem, bound for two different paths. He hadn't even known those paths had a common thread until three months ago. Or that without his help, that thread entered the world only nine short months after he left for boot camp, seaming them together with a stitch tighter and more substantial than some long-put-aside young love. He didn't know that fact six years ago, and in all honesty, he didn't know with total confidence whether he wanted to know it now.

The silver maples lining Main Street flickered, now bearing the unremarkable colors of burnt sienna on their underbellies. A few fell like feathers against the pavement as he came to a stop at the corner light of the courthouse square.

He'd trained for some of the most mentally and physically challenging conditions endurable as a Marine Raider, but no special ops training in the world could have shored him up for the mission he had now in the little spot in the world called Camden Grove.

Businesses lined the streets like a variety of stacked cereal boxes—The Herbs Shoppe, Cash and Carry, a dime store with frontage that looked like it hadn't seen change since the 50's. Baker's Hardware showcased a bright red snow sled in its window for the wishful kids of a snowless town too far south.

As he rounded the square, a little shop with a fashionably distressed sign advertising Dawson's Creamery caught his attention. It seemed a likely place to start looking. Maybe he could get a cup of coffee there, too. Though it wasn't his drink of choice, he wanted something a little stouter to cinch up his nerves than the watered-down soda in his cup holder.

The whole way to Camden Grove from North Carolina had left him in a tumult about how to confront Paige. He'd summoned every scenario he could imagine, worked through all her responses in his head. His job had taught him to cover every contingency before he approached a volatile situation, but this wasn't some military exercise. It was much closer to home. He had no idea how she would react. He'd been trained to assume the worst.

If he'd known out of the gate that another living human with his DNA was on the horizon, maybe things would have been different back then. He had arguably loved Paige. Other things had just claimed him long before she did. That, and he'd been deceived.

With the distance of six years, they'd both gone on with their lives.

Maybe by now, she had somebody new in her life. Likely, she did. He suspected she wasn't married, though. His search had led to evidence that she still used her maiden name. Whether or not that was a reliable indicator, something in him hoped she wasn't in a relationship. It would make his visit less complicated.

Tapping the wheel, he waited for a car to vacate a parking spot.

He just needed to make her understand he wasn't a deadbeat. Maybe if he told her the truth—that only recently he'd found out about their daughter—from there, he could offer whatever financial help was his responsibility to handle, be as passive a parent as she likely wanted him to be, and return to the life he'd built in the service. Get in, do the job, and get out. It was the way of a Raider.

He pulled into the diagonal parking space in front of the Creamery beside a pickup the likes of which he might've seen at a juiced-up truck show. The hydraulics propped the cab at an angle as if it were ready to bounce to its cranked audio.

The door of the shop jingled as he entered, and at two small, joined tables in the front of the store, a group of teenagers huddled in a mumbling cluster.

They each scanned Maddox as he passed their table. He sensed them sizing him up. He was a stranger in their neck of the woods.

"Maybe she can get a date with *him*." One of the girls laughed. She'd spoken loudly enough to be overheard.

A quarterback-sized kid with a letterman jacket sitting center stage didn't care if he was heard or not. "No way. He's got to be thirty somethin'. Nobody over twenty wears denim shirts anymore. He might as well be sportin' Velcro shoes and have food in his teeth."

Giggles burst into full-scale cackling as Maddox glanced over his shoulder toward the group.

The second girl, whose fake eyelashes matched the length of her acrylic nails, found a need to contribute. "He's not half bad looking, though, so, yeah, you're probably right . . . no chance."

A mirrored logo hung against the wall of the shop opposite the huddled group. Maddox turned away from them and watched their reflection as the three boys bumped fists. The jeers and squeals died down to a mumble as the young girl behind the counter approached Maddox at the cash register. She wore a pink T-shirt and a matching visor. The embroidered slogan on each read, *I've got the scoop at Dawson's Creamery.*

"Can I help you?" she muttered, her face bent against her tormentors. Unmistakable splotches of red beneath her eyes confirmed what Maddox already suspected.

"Just a cup of coffee." He pulled out his wallet and glanced a second time at the group through the reflective logo.

When she set the steaming Styrofoam cup on the counter in front of him, he put a five down and shoved the change she gave him in the tips cup beside the cash register.

"Thanks." He gestured with the lift of his cup, then leaned in, noting her name tag. "So . . . Gabby . . . since you've got the scoop around here, you wouldn't know a woman named Paige Westerfield who lives in the area, would you?" He felt his *denim* shirt pocket. He'd forgotten the old photo in the console of the Jeep.

The girl never looked up, but shook her head and wiped down the counter.

Maddox persisted. "She has a little girl, about five years old. I thought they might come in every once in a while."

"We have a lot of people with little kids come into the store, mister."

"I have a photo I could show you. It's just in the—"

"It wouldn't really matter." The girl cut off his comment. "I don't pay much attention to what people look like."

Maddox nodded at the top of the girl's head, her chin tucked low. "Right. Thanks anyway."

The banter behind him had never stopped. He turned and made his way to a booths with a sure view and, after a few seconds of sipping on his steaming cup, pulled out his phone and began recording. Why he did it, he didn't really know. He'd planned to come into town, keep his nose to the task, and take care of business, but something about helping the underdog had been one reason he'd become a Marine. The girl behind the counter? She was in an underdog situation, if he'd ever seen one. And the bully mentality never had set right with him.

Oblivious to his observation, the teens at the two tables howled with another prod at the girl's expense. She set her cloth in the basin behind the counter and retreated to the farthest corner of the shop.

After a few more minutes, Maddox stood and tossed his half-empty cup in the waste bin. Walking toward the door, he told himself the whole time he should leave well enough alone, but, when the whiny voice of Lashes and Nails pierced his ear with a snide "I told you she didn't have a chance," he stopped in his tracks.

Stepping up to their table, Maddox didn't give them time to wonder why he was there. "You know, what you're doing is not cool."

The girls' giggles melted into annoyed smirks. Quarterback cocked his head and threw a glare at Maddox. "What business is it of yours?"

"I'm just asking you to stop."

"Ask away, but that won't get you very far."

Get in. Get the job done. Get out. Maddox took a deep breath. He'd wanted to come into town quietly. Something told him this was going to get loud. "One of you guys own that hopped-up truck out there?"

Quarterback raised his eyebrows, confused at first. Then he nodded with a sneer of pride. "That's mine."

"Some kinda ride you got there. How much did you pay for it?"

The kid's expression turned from pride to contempt. He hesitated, eyes narrowing in sleepy defiance. "A lot."

Maddox smiled, his voice as calm as a rippling brook. "You don't know how much because you didn't pay for it. Daddy buy that for you? Did his boy need an ego stroke to compensate for his shortage of brains?" Maddox did the sizing up this time, scanning Quarterback and friends with a look of boredom.

The smiles around the table straightened to shock. Lashes and Nails nearly dropped her fountain drink between her talons as Quarterback stood up, shoving his chair across the floor.

Maddox casually shrugged his shoulders, turned, and walked out.

Before he got past the front of the truck outside, the door of the shop behind him slammed open, rattling its metal frame. From the sound of the girls' clicking heels, Quarterback and his followers spilled out of the shop onto the sidewalk behind him. Maddox caught sight of the ringleader reflected in the chrome of his truck's grill.

The kid started toward Maddox in a run.

Within an inch of contact, Maddox turned, caught the boy's punch in his hand, twisted his arm behind him, and shoved him face down to the hood of his own truck. The kid's face contorted. Maddox then set his phone in front of the boy's nose and played the clip he'd recorded inside. As their voices howled with laughter from the phone's speaker, Quarterback's friends stood against the wall of the store as if they'd been chained there.

Maddox drew close to the boy's ear. "This," he tapped on the phone, "is called harassment." The jeers and squeals from the footage came after each abuse they'd inflicted on the girl inside. "Not only is it grounds for you to lose that football scholarship you've most likely got lined up, but it's also plenty of motivation for legal action if my niece in there should take offense at things like I do."

Maddox had become proficient at persuasion with all his training. He'd also mastered the use of necessary lies when they were told for the benefit of a mission. In the last 15 minutes, as sorry as it was, this had become the small-town version of a mission. Nevermind that it was a sidestep to the one he'd originally set out to complete.

With little effort, he held the boy in place as he tried to move beneath his weight. It was a shame the kid didn't have the self-respect of a jarhead. He could probably have been a decent private with a little discipline.

The kid wiggled some more. "Man, I didn't know she was your niece!"

"Should that matter?" Maddox waited for an answer, then encouraged one with a little nudge at the boy's shoulder blade.

"No," he yelped. "No. Okay? You satisfied?"

"Not really. In fact, I suggest that you and your buddies go inside, apologize, and then find another after-school hangout. Sound like a good idea to you? And if you or any of your friends give so much as a cross look to Gabby in the future, I guess I'll have to show that clip around until I find somebody who cares."

He nudged the Quarterback's shoulder again until he called out to the others, "Apologize to her!" he panted. "Dude's gonna break my arm."

The group of teens ran back inside as Maddox dropped the boy from the hood. "That was a little dramatic, don't you think? I still had a good thirty pounds of pressure before it would've snapped."

"You could be arrested for assault!" Quarterback spewed his fury, then wiped his mouth with the back of his hand.

"You're not having the best of luck with recordings today." Maddox calmly pointed across the street. "My bet is those cameras over there at the hardware store would tell a different story. Convenient, that they're pointed right this way. Didn't you come at me with my back turned?" He nodded at the Creamery door. "You should go on and take care of business."

The boy disappeared inside as the others spilled back out of the shop and scattered. Maddox waited in the Jeep.

When Quarterback returned, he cut Maddox a noxious look. Then, without further suggestion, he jumped in his truck and squealed tires toward the east side of the square, leaving a set of black streaks in his wake.

Maddox leaned back against the headrest and closed his eyes, trying to refocus on the reason he'd come to Camden Grove in the first place. He didn't have time to clear his thoughts before the girl from the shop stepped outside and walked up to the passenger-side door. She looked into his eyes for the first time. "You're not my uncle."

Maddox dropped his gaze. "No, but they didn't know that, and if I did have a niece, I'd want her to be treated right."

A smile twitched to life beneath her blotchy, red eyes. "Thanks . . . Well, the next time you come in, the coffee and a scoop of ice cream's on me." She turned to go inside, but then stepped back. "Hey, that lady you're looking for. What's her name again?"

Maddox took a deep breath. "Paige Westerfield."

"You're not any kind of stalker, are you?" The girl gave him a cautious glance.

Maddox shook his head and grinned. The memory of a similar question from long ago colored his thoughts. "She'd probably say I'd forgotten her altogether. We lost contact a few years back, but I found out she moved here recently." He pulled the worn photo from the console and handed it to her. "This is an old picture, but any chance you might've seen her around?"

"She's pretty." The girl hesitated. "Yeah, I've seen her. She comes in with a little girl every once in a while. Seems nice. I had to go with my mom to the doctor's office about a month ago. She works there. It's the new place down on Brewster Street off the south end of the main drag. I think she's an office worker." She handed the photo back.

"Thanks, Gabby."

"Yeah." She stepped back. "See you around."

After she opened the shop door and disappeared inside, Maddox glanced again at the photo. Two younger versions of himself and Paige filled the frame with guarded smiles.

He tucked the photo in a seam of the dashboard, gripped the steering wheel with an anxious hand, and put the Jeep in reverse. Stopping at the ice cream shop had been a stroke of luck, one he could only hope would continue. As he drove onto Main Street and picked up speed, the photo quivered against the dashboard, and he tried for the hundredth time to shake off the lingering shock of the truth that on the night he'd snapped that photo, his daughter was conceived.

Chapter Two

Paige

Paige counted her move to Camden Grove as one of the best things that had ever happened for her on the heels of enough hard years to last a lifetime. By her twenty-fifth birthday, she had already seen dispossession by an unsympathetic family; the birth of her daughter, Emmie, when she was too young to know how to care for her; and the struggles of finding a way for her and a baby with special needs to survive entirely alone. She'd always had to be resourceful, but being capable and superhuman were two different things.

A few months back, when the sky opened and an angel descended in the form of her employer, Dr. Ava Fenn, she counted her good fortune as a miracle in a time when she thought they'd ceased to exist.

Ava welcomed Paige and Emmie like family when they moved to the Grove. She, her fiancé Logan, his son Toby, and a couple of local photographers Carly and Jessie created a close-knit group around the two. With their newfound friendships, Paige had finally shed some of the loneliness that had plagued her before she came here.

Sometimes, she was afraid to hope that life could get better. Getting Emmie enrolled in kindergarten and herself signed up for online classes had provided some needed structure in their first weeks at the Grove. Still, a new place, a new schedule, and new responsibilities didn't come without trials.

Separation anxiety caused more morning cries for Paige and Emmie than she wanted to admit, but she knew that having her little girl engaged with other children was important. And the spunky five-year-old had survived the first trying years of her childhood with the heart of a champion. Her stubbornness—what one of Emmie's doctors had been insensitive enough to call a "character flaw" of children with Down syndrome—had served her well so many times. How else were they supposed to get through tough times but with sheer grit?

At the end of the day, at the close of the workweek, Paige sat at her desk and breathed a sigh of contentment, the office now quiet. Everyone had already left, ready for the weekend, and after riding in from school with Logan and Toby, Emmie had gone, with headphones and a tablet in hand, to the kitchenette for a snack.

With a moment to catch her breath, Paige stared at the photo on her desk. The only professional shot she owned of her daughter and her, Carly had snapped it a couple of months after they'd arrived in Camden Grove and put it in a frame as a welcome gift. Her little girl's eyes sparkled in the photo as she stood behind Paige, arms wrapped around her neck, her thin brown wisps of hair trailing onto Paige's shoulders.

Paige loved that picture. The first thing she saw was a happy little girl. Likely not what everyone else initially noticed about Emmie. More often than she'd have liked, Down syndrome spoke to people from the shapes of her eyes, long before they could see past that to the joy.

Finally, with a glance at the clock, she cleared her desk of an invoice, placing it in the inbox for her attention on Monday, and began putting the remaining pens, sticky notes, and paper clips away in the drawer. Everything in its place at the end of the day gave her a simple satisfaction, like she'd tied up all the loose ends.

When the front office door opened, Paige didn't look up at first. "Sorry, the doctor just left, and I was about to lock—"

As she raised her eyes to the visitor, she nearly dropped the handful of paper clips. From her spot behind the counter, she looked directly into the eyes of the man she thought she'd never see again. Her breath caught in her throat.

He hesitated at first. Then his voice, deeper now, more coarse than she remembered, called her name, "Paige?"

Her mouth went dry, and her heart pounded against her chest like someone had suddenly jump-started it. She hadn't heard her name cross his lips for six years.

Slipping from her desk, leaving the paper clips in a tangled pile, she was now more conscious of the photo of her and Emmie than before. She put herself in front of it. The last thing she wanted him to see right now was that their smiles so naturally matched.

The words almost didn't come at first. Like combing through wool, she tugged to make sounds from her thoughts. "Wh-what're you doing here?"

Maddox stepped closer. His face looked sharper than when she'd last seen him, his chiseled cheekbones now more prominently framing the top of a squared jawline. Close-shorn hair faded into a precise military cut, a shade or two darker than she remembered. His shoulders were no longer those of a leaner high-school boy. They had broadened, and his chest had thickened. The arms beneath his clothing bulged as he fidgeted with a key fob in his hands.

"How are you?" His voice wavered.

Paige tried to reign in the thoughts running helter-skelter through her head, struggled without effect to shake off the shock. She finally rounded her shoulders. "Are you still . . . enlisted?"

To most, that question would have seemed benign, strange even, but it was a feeble attempt on her part to cut to the quick the man in front of her. She'd spent six years crafting an arsenal of caustic thoughts for the unlikely day she could take aim and fire, but now that he stood just feet away, she couldn't think of a single thing more biting to say.

He nodded and fumbled more with the key fob now wrapped around his ring finger. "Yes." He paused, then repeated, "How are you?"

An afflicted half chuckle slipped from her mouth, but she didn't respond with anything more, just kept staring at him.

He stepped closer again, leaned with hands propped on the counter toward the receptionist's window. "Look, I know this must be a little shocking, me coming into town like this—"

"How did you find me?" Paige cut him off with the sharpness of her voice.

"I've been looking for you." Maddox bowed his head. "Did some digging and happened across your name in an article about that doctor that was indicted back in Nashville. Didn't take too much to follow the trail here."

"I wasn't involved in that mess in Nashville." She snapped. "Other than to help put him away."

"No, I wasn't suggesting . . ." He paused, then tried to lighten the mood. "Looks like a pretty nice town." He pointed a thumb back toward the door. "I stopped by the little ice cream shop on the way in. Met some of the local kids."

Paige turned away, pulled her sweater from the back of the office chair, and slipped the photo frame face down. "I should really close up here."

"That her?" He pointed to the frame.

Paige pulled her purse over her shoulder. "What're you talking about?"

"In the photo?"

"Look, I have to get to my other responsibilities."

"Do they include our daughter?" His words, abrupt and true, stopped Paige cold in her tracks. She stood with her back to Maddox, trying to find air. She could hear the ticking of the clock on the wall in front of her—like a time bomb, that ticking.

"I know about her, Paige. Our daughter."

"You have no right to call her that." She spun around, her lip trembling with every word. "You don't know anything. But you should. I only wrote a hundred times, hoping you'd write back, praying you'd call—anything." She stopped and tried to control her breathing. "So, overlook my ignorance if I don't really understand why you're coming around now."

Maddox rubbed the back of his neck. "Is there a place we can talk for a while?"

"No." She fumbled with her sweater. "I've got to go."

"I didn't know, Paige." He let out an exasperated breath. "I just found out what happened three months ago."

"What do you mean you just found out?" Anger burned a trail up her throat.

"I'd like to sit down and talk with you awhile." He stroked his jaw. "A lot needs saying."

Not knowing whether to be more shocked at his actually being there or at what he was telling her, she stood rooted to the floor in silence. Then, in an effort to compose herself, she opened the desk drawer and swept the tangle of paper clips inside. "Things that needed saying six years ago?"

"That and a lot more."

"I've had to wait, Maddox. Sounds like you could stand a lesson in waiting, too." She crossed to the receptionist's window and slammed it shut, almost catching his hand in the tracks.

"Please, Paige. Can't we just talk?"

She fixed her grip tighter on the straps of her purse. "No, we can't."

"Paige, look at me." He set his hand against the glass. "Look at me," he spoke louder, pleading.

She stopped and glared directly into the topaz blue eyes she'd tried so long to forget.

"I know you need time for this to . . . sink in." He opened his mouth as if to say something, then must have thought better of it. "I'll be staying at the bed-and-breakfast on the other side of town. I'll be there when you're ready to talk." He gave her one last lingering look and stepped away. As the door closed behind him, the leaves from the peace lily in the waiting room quivered with the incoming breeze.

Paige sat back down in the office chair, her knees weak, the purse sliding from her shoulder. "I may never be ready to talk," she whispered.

Her hands still trembled when Emmie came in from the kitchenette, pulling the headphones from her ears.

"Mommy. Are we. Going home?" Emmie's short and halting speech had been a language characteristic the doctors had prepared Paige for early on. It was simply Emmie's voice, but now, after the shock of seeing Maddox, it seemed more noticeable. Emmie's hair bounced as she rounded the desk and saw the photo frame lying flat. "Hey. Did this. Fall down?" She lifted it and set it prominently back in its spot on the desk corner.

"Yes, sweetheart, we're going home."

After Paige locked the front entry, Emmie shuffled behind with her oversized school bag claiming the better part of her back. "Can we have. Pizza tonight?"

Paige ignored Emmie's question and held her hand as they exited the rear door of the office. She glanced toward the front of the building, half expecting to see Maddox, but the lot was empty. He was gone.

Chapter Three

Maddox

Mulligans' Bed-and-Breakfast stood on the corner of Main Street a few blocks from the square. The towering Victorian house seemed out of place, the only structure of its kind in a community with buildings of a half-century more recent construction. The facades of many of the businesses in town had metal placards claiming development in the 50s and 60s, and most of the ranch houses along the main route looked as if they'd been constructed at the same time by the same builder—like the whole town had been born on the same day.

Maddox parked the Jeep in front of a detached garage, pulled his sea bag from the back seat, and made a slow approach to the front porch, taking in the ornate details of the house. The steep, gabled roof had castle-top shingles and a turret that ran up the sunset corner. Round angles and shapely windows added a soft contrast to the pointy spire at the top of the turret. He stepped onto the porch, skirted with a decorative, spindled banister, and only then noticed someone close by.

"You'll not find the lady inside to take your money. And the money she likes to take, bless 'er. Though she'd sooner take mine than yours." The throaty sounds of an Irishman wound round the side of the house as an old man's face appeared at the eve next to the porch ceiling.

Stepping back to gain a better view, Maddox cupped his hand over his brow to block the light of the setting sun. The old man stood on a ladder, swiping leaves and debris from the gutters.

"A minute more, and I can finish the job. I'll be down to help ye then." As the man emptied the last of the leaves into a garbage bag attached to the ladder, he eased to the ground, the speed of his descent clearly slowed by the stiffness in his limbs.

"Ah," he let out an exasperated sigh. "These old bones, they creak and moan, to be sure." He brushed his hand on his brown corduroy pants and held it over the banister for a shake. "Hugh Mulligan. No need for misters or sirs as they like to do 'round here. Just Hugh. And you would be?"

"Maddox. Maddox Granger." He shook the old man's hand.

"Granger. Granger." The man spoke to himself as if he were combing through his thoughts. "An English name, I do believe. And if I recall, I've run across it a few times in the searching. Not like the Smiths or Joneses around here, though, mind ye."

"Searching?" Maddox raised his eyebrows.

"Family Tree. It's my love, 'tis . . . well, besides the little lady." He rounded the corner of the banister and climbed the four steps of the porch. "And Granger is an English name, but I won't hold it against ye now." He cackled. "Come, let's have a gargle."

Maddox followed the man as he shuffled into the house, the inside of which they'd decorated with trinkets undoubtedly as old as the structure itself.

"Sorry, the little woman lets me get by with only things of mild nature now. I can put some coffee on, but the spike of Irish cream would be just a figment, I'm afraid."

Maddox nodded. "No, thanks. I was wanting to rent a room."

The old man shuffled to the far side of the front parlor to a small table with a vintage coffee maker. "You're a tame one then, are ye?" He bent to a small refrigerator in the corner and pulled out a cold bottle of water.

As he handed over the drink, he pointed toward a chair. "Sit. We can visit. My Glenna went to the store. She'll come back in short order. She handles all the business, she does." He poured what must have been the stiff remainder of morning coffee from the bottom of the glass pot and eased with a grunt into a velveteen wingback across from Maddox. "What branch of service are ye in?"

"Marines."

"Haircut. Dog tag 'round your neck. You're a fit one. And that olive drab sea bag gives ye away if nary another thing does."

Maddox's eyes landed on the bag at his feet.

The old man sipped his coffee. "All that, and I can smell the angst on ye. I served myself once, ye know. Irish Army, 32nd Battalion."

Maddox took a new interest. "Where were you stationed?"

"The Congo for a good bit." The man's eyes, slanted with the weight of age, lost their momentary sparkle. "I was in the patrol caught in the Ambush. Niemba Ambush."

"Don't think I've heard of it."

"You wouldn't have. Yer a young'un." He smiled and bowed his head. "I may tell ye about it, should ye stay a while."

A squeak from the spring of a back door indicated that Mrs. Mulligan had returned. When she entered the room, Maddox and Hugh stood, the older kissing his bride on the forehead and Maddox waiting for introductions.

"Glenna dear, this is Maddox Granger. He's come to let a room."

The woman, wrapped in a lightweight, red poncho, patted her husband on the arm, then met Maddox with her hand extended. She squeezed his warmly as she held it still. "Well, hello there." Her deep southern drawl was a stark contrast to Hugh's lilting Irish sounds. "So good you came to visit with us."

"Mrs. Mulligan, nice to meet you." Maddox tipped his head.

She waved off the formalities. "Honey, if you're staying here with us, there's one rule. We treat people like family. So, you need to call me Glenna. Now, what brings you to the Grove?" She released his hand and slipped the poncho over her head. A few loose strands of gray, pinned-up hair popped with static.

"I came to visit somebody I used to know a few years back." Maddox set the water bottle beside his sea bag and drew his wallet from his back pocket. "I'm not sure yet how long I'll need a room, but it'll at least be a couple of days."

"Of course." She moved toward a corner coat rack. "Let me just put this away, and I'll get you a key." She turned toward Hugh. "Should we put him in the Blue Room, sweetie?"

"The Blue Room's a perfect choice, love."

Maddox hid a slight grin as he listened to the odd exchange of deeply dripping southern *honeys* and *sweeties* against Hugh's quicker and sharper Irish affections.

The woman disappeared around a corner toward the back of the house, but was no sooner gone than she'd returned with a skeleton key the size of Maddox's index finger.

Hugh set his coffee cup on the desk and shuffled to the drawer, pulling out a register.

"Oh, Hugh"—Glenna waved the air again as if to shoo a fly—"let's save that for later since we don't know how long he'll be here."

The old man nodded obediently.

She glanced at the wallet in Maddox's hand. "You put that away. We'll take care of business when business is done." She smiled.

After Hugh tucked the register back into the drawer, he pointed to the clock, "We eat breakfast promptly at eight in the morn, but should ye have need for quick eats or a bit of sustenance, Glenna stocks the guest cooler with plenty of treats and in-betweens. We'll show ye around a bit and take ye to your room, but ye must take in the conservatory and garden at some point. They're the jewels of the house." With the beckoning of a hand, he urged Maddox to follow him and Glenna on the tour.

As they walked, the Mulligans talked of the origins of furniture, historic cracks in the moldings, and the sites of various momentous events throughout the house's long history. When they ultimately came to the Blue Room, Maddox understood the reason behind the name. Everything from the upholstery to the bed linens, the wall colors to the stationary on the corner roll-top desk claimed its place on the color wheel in some hue of blue.

"Here ye are, m'boy." Hugh patted him on the back.

"The Blue Room." Maddox nodded.

"Glenna always has a good sense of what our guests need as they stay here." He stepped into the room. "Ye must be one that requires some peace."

"And blue is such a tranquil color, don't you think, Maddox?" Glenna tilted her head to the side. Without waiting for a response, she signaled to Hugh. "We should leave him to get his things unpacked, darlin'." To Maddox, she pointed. "And when you have a spell, be sure to come to the conservatory. It's just through the breakfast room. Like Hugh says, it's a hidden gem."

"Thank you. I'll have to do that." He gave a quick nod.

Glenna handed over the key, and she and Hugh eased the door closed, leaving Maddox to his thoughts.

Alone in the room, he set his seabag on the diamond-tufted bench at the end of the bed and took a seat beside it. Images of what had transpired in his first few hours in Camden Grove bombarded his thoughts: the bullies in the ice cream shop; the cashier named Gabby and her red, blotchy face; the old Irishman and the diminished sparkle in his eye when he mentioned the Congo; and his wife's handshake as warm as a grandmother's.

All those thoughts swirled like a twister in his head, but caught in the storm's eye sat one prevailing image: Paige at the office and her expression when she first laid eyes on him.

He drew in a deep breath in an effort to dismiss them all.

Blue. He looked around. Blue everywhere. But Glenna was right. Something about the color seemed calming and was a welcome break from the bland neutrals of life at Camp Lejeune.

As Maddox unpacked his seabag, he filled one drawer in the corner wardrobe with his clothes, hung his jacket on a hook inside the door, and set a folder on the bed before tucking his bag beneath it. At least the room had the modern amenity of a television. He pulled a pillow from under the spread, leaned against the headboard, and punched a button on the remote.

For a moment, he lay there with the droning voice of a newscaster eulogizing a recent supreme court decision. But with the folder lying next to him, all he really heard was the voice of his father, the Colonel, ringing in his ears.

Semper Fi, son. Semper Fi.

The Latin translation meant *Always Faithful.* For every other recruit, it was the rally cry for loyalty, honor, and commitment as a Marine. But for Maddox, it was a veiled reminder from the Colonel to keep focused on following in his footsteps. He'd wanted his son's uniform decorated with metal—*a chest of fruit salad*, his buddies would say. But when Maddox had made the cut as a Raider against the Colonel's wishes, the reminders stopped.

With little pomp and circumstance, the Raider motto *Always Faithful, Always Forward* took the place of *Semper Fi,* and the additional call to overcome challenges and accomplish objectives became his lodestar.

Now, even those words held a layered meaning. Since his father's death and the news that came with it only three short months ago, not only did he have cause to consider loyalty, honor, and commitment, but he wondered what forward momentum really looked like.

The Colonel's funeral had prompted the unforeseen conversation with his mother afterward, one that changed everything, caused him to question everything. That's when *Always Faithful, Always Forward* became an expectation that haunted him more than motivated him. And the thought of his father reeling off *Semper Fi,* like some manipulative chant, made his stomach sour with bitterness.

As the newscaster segued to a new story, Maddox pulled the collection of papers out of the folder and laid them on the bed beside him. The heading at the top of the first page taunted him: *DD Form 4—Enlistment/Reenlistment Document.*

Three months earlier, the decision would have been open-and-shut, and, for all practical purposes, it still was. He was part of a team of men who worked together like a machine in perfect sync. The Marine mindset was practically laced into his DNA. From toddlerhood, the Colonel had branded into Maddox's mind stories of their family members leading battle in every major theater on the planet. He constantly preached notions of Maddox continuing the family legacy.

Maddox had always embraced the path of a serviceman, but he'd bucked at the military-college approach the Colonel had proposed. Instead, he opted to enlist fresh out of high school with the quiet goal of becoming a Raider. It was why he'd signed up initially for six years instead of the standard four. The selection process for MARSOC, or the Marine Special Ops Command, didn't even begin until after year three.

Hard as it was to leave Paige after enlistment, he knew his path and what it required. He had hopes of reuniting with her after he got a good start.

Some hopes just don't materialize, though.

Lying there in the comfort of the Blue Room, he thought about all the men on his team. Bailey and Lamberg, Pate and Gillings, Tigler and Stokes. Not one wouldn't lay down his life for the others. They had fused bonds under the heat of combat, ties that would never be severed.

In his three years as a Raider, he'd found his brotherhood, hit his stride. But he couldn't deny that now, as he sat in a blue room in the little town of Camden Grove staring at the papers to re-up, something nagged at him. He let that nagging work into his head enough for a question to slip in: what would *not* being a Raider look like?

Felt almost traitorous even thinking it.

He held a breath, trying to refocus.

A few hours before he'd left Camp Lejeune, he told Tigler and Stokes where he was going. Of all his comrades, he was closest to them.

Stokes, a west coast surfer who'd cut his teeth on barrels and pipelines, and Tigler, an Idaho farm boy, no stranger to long days and calloused hands, had ended up on the same detail with Maddox when they'd endured the first three weeks of Assessment and Selection together. They'd all cemented their friendship a few weeks later in water survival when Stokes coached him and Tigler on the off hours about how to avoid drowning under the determined hands of their trainers.

When Maddox shared with them his plans to come to Camden Grove and why, like brothers, they'd backed him a hundred percent. *Always faithful, always forward.* He wondered what they'd say if they knew he even entertained a passing question in his head about re-upping. Probably would have never crossed their minds. He was too much a stalwart.

The abrupt switch from the newscast to a commercial pulled Maddox's thoughts back to the papers. Frustrated, he slapped the folder shut. He'd look at them later.

Other things demanded headspace now. His short time in this town had brought him no closer to an answer about how to handle the recent developments in his life than he'd been before he came to Camden Grove. No more able to reconcile how an old flame and the DNA of a little girl somewhere across town could stir up so much anxiety.

On Saturday, Maddox hesitated to leave the bed-and-breakfast, thinking that maybe Paige would stop by the Mulligans' to talk. But since he wasn't staying at a bed-and-breakfast-lunch-and-dinner, he had to make his way out at some point. Around noon, he drove into town and got word from the locals that the barbecue place they called Wiggs' was an essential stop for visitors to Camden Grove. Mouth-watering. That's what they'd called it.

The place didn't look like any restaurant he'd seen along the coast. The gray metal building reminded him remotely of the grain bins he'd passed on the way into town, but with a more modern flair, and definitely cleaner. Red shutters framed out the windows with a bright touch, and the barn-style doors completed the look to make it a welcoming enough place.

He smelled the barbecue from the moment he pulled into the parking lot. And when he stepped inside, the line was backed up to the door, confirming that the locals' bragging must be justified.

As the line inched closer to the ordering counter, a couple of men, who looked like twin brothers, chit-chatted in front of Maddox until their conversation lulled, and one casually turned, addressing him directly.

"You must be new around here. I don't think I've seen you before."

"Me?" Maddox raised an eyebrow. "No, I'm from out of town."

The line continued to move closer to the woman taking orders.

"Just passing through, then? Where you headed?" the other of the two men asked.

"Actually, I'm staying here for a few days."

"You've found the right place to get a bite to eat, then," the first twin replied.

"So I've heard."

"Name's Wyatt, and this jokester's my brother, Logan. Least, that's what I call him. I think he was adopted."

The other one rolled his eyes. "If I had a dollar for every time he made that stupid comment, I could've retired by now." He held out a hand to shake.

"Nice to meet you. Name's Maddox." He offered the expected pleasantries, but he wasn't really in the mood to chat.

"You military?" the one who called himself Wyatt asked.

"You're the second person in town who's guessed that."

"We parked outside just before you. The Department of Defense parking sticker gave you away." The other one—Logan—moved forward another step.

"Guess if I wanted to keep a low profile, I shouldn't advertise, huh?" Maddox shoved his hands into his pockets.

"Good luck with that. Small town like this?" Wyatt nodded at the crowd in the dining area. "I guarantee there's a good handful of people here who already had you pegged about three seconds after you came through the door."

With a scan of the room, Maddox could see a few people had taken notice of him. He changed the subject. "What's good to eat here?"

"Not a bad plate in the house." Logan picked up a to-go menu from a box holder mounted to the wall and handed it to Maddox. "But I hear Wiggs has kahlua pork this week. He's already testing out a few new recipes for the luau he throws every year."

He talked of the owner as if he knew him well. But then, it sounded like everybody knew everybody in Camden Grove.

As they stepped up to the woman at the counter, Logan called her by name and placed his order. When he and his brother got their plates, they turned toward the dining room, where a worker wiped down the last available table. Logan called over his shoulder toward Maddox. "Full house, looks like. When you get your plate, come and join us."

Before Maddox could answer, Logan had already turned and headed for the empty table. He hesitated at first, but then, he really didn't have anywhere else to be. Maybe getting acquainted with a few of the locals wouldn't be so bad. Talking to people besides Raiders hadn't been in his scope of things to do lately.

He glanced around as he waited for his order. Red picnic tables decked in checkered plastic tablecloths held families, work crews, business types, and a few college-aged kids. The noise from the crowd rumbled over Elvis singing "Blue Hawaii" from the jukebox in the corner. And against the walls, rows of business cards lined the slatted, raw timbers—even more evidence of the restaurant's popularity. The place seemed almost homey. A strange mix between the islands and the deep South, but homey, nonetheless.

When Maddox slid onto the bench across from the men, they were already in conversation.

"Yeah, I'll be finishing up that project next week, then I've got to do the prep work on Carly and Jessie's billboard campaign. You'll be up in lights in no time, my man." Wyatt nodded at his brother.

"You in advertising or something?" Maddox asked.

"Yeah, and this dude here is the model I've got to work with the next few weeks." He pointed a thumb at Logan. "Tragedy, huh? They should've picked me since I'm the better-looking one."

"Again, if I had a dollar." Logan squirted extra barbecue sauce on his plate from a half-empty squeeze bottle.

Maddox grinned. The two bantering back and forth reminded him of the baiting among him, Tigler, and Stokes. Always giving each other what for was how he knew he could trust them, how he knew everything was right in the world. When they got quiet? That's when something was serious enough to worry about.

The locals were right. The barbecue *was* mouthwatering, some of the best he'd ever had. All three of the men sat enjoying their meals as the conversation hit a lull.

"So, what are you advertising?" Maddox asked between bites.

Logan pulled a napkin from a roll of paper towels perched on a stand close by and wiped his mouth. "A few months back, I was fortunate enough to meet the woman I'll be marrying before long.

And somehow, this clown got the job of putting our photos on a billboard advertising a bridal fair over in Hartley."

Wyatt pointed his fork at his brother. "I set up Romeo here with the woman of his dreams, and he calls me a clown. Let's not mention that she happens to be the doctor in town. So, the woman's brilliant, *and* she's a babe. But brother gets no credit for that, does he?"

Maddox's ears perked up. In a town this size, there couldn't reasonably be more than one doctor. "Is she the one in the office down on Brewster?"

"Yeah, you know her?" Logan asked.

"Oh, no, not the doctor. I just stopped there yesterday for . . . directions. Talked to the receptionist." He picked at his plate with the fork. "She . . . reminded me of somebody I knew a long time ago."

"Paige? Yeah, she's a good gal. She and her daughter are new in town. Just moved to the Grove from Nashville a while back."

Wyatt added, "A hard worker, that one. Raising her daughter by herself. Going to school. Working a full-time job. I don't know too many women with that kind of moxie."

"Sounds right," Maddox said to himself more than to them.

Wyatt and Logan looked at him.

"I mean, you'd have to be hardworking to take on all that responsibility at once, right?"

"No joke." Logan took a sip of his drink. "She's got a pretty great kid, though. I think that's a lot of her motivation."

"Oh, yeah?" Maddox cued his voice to a tone of subtle interest.

"Yeah, her little girl plays with my boy Toby quite a lot. They've become big friends since she came to town. Toby has type 1 diabetes, and Emmie has Down syndrome. So, they watch out for each other."

The statement came as a gut punch to Maddox. It was the first time he'd ever heard his daughter's name.

Then, an instant later, the words Down syndrome registered in his head. He tuned out most everything else from that moment on, nodding only when a response seemed appropriate. And even though the meal was delicious, he barely picked at the rest of it.

After a few more minutes, he made an excuse, thanked the men for sharing a table, and left them where they sat.

For the next hour, Maddox drove some of the rural highways on the outskirts of town, trying to gain perspective. He was just beginning to wrap his head around the fact that he had a daughter. The thought had never crossed his mind that she might have special needs. He tried to talk himself through whether that made a difference, attempted to convince himself it didn't.

The longer he drove, the more Paige's words played in his head.

I wrote a hundred times . . .

Hoping you'd write back . . .

Praying you'd call. . . .

He didn't know whether to be more upset that until a short time ago, he had no idea about Emmie and hadn't been able to make choices based on that knowledge or that, if he had known about everything, he might well have deserved Paige's lack of faith in him.

He gripped the steering wheel.

It was all territory he'd never crossed.

Along a broad stretch of farmland, Maddox finally pulled the Jeep off the road to the edge of a field. Bolls of leftover cotton littered the edge of the harvested cropland like the remnants of melting snow. As he scanned the picked rows, stubbled and brown, frustration welled up inside him.

Again and again, he questioned whether he'd have thought longer and harder about finding Paige had he known everything. If he were honest, he didn't yet know. If he were direct, not much scared him, but everything about this did.

He'd never been around a soul with special needs. From high-school sports to the military, from childhood to adulthood, the top of the top were his crowd. And he'd had to scratch tooth and nail to earn every second being on that list among them. What did he know of how to act around a child in the first place? But a child . . . like Emmie? And what could he say to Paige?

He sat at the field's edge until an old farmer pulled off the road in his rusty pickup to ask if Maddox was having problems. After dispelling the old man's curiosities, he started the Jeep and headed back toward town, still no closer to answers than he had been in the days before he came to Camden Grove. Probably further from.

Twenty minutes later, as he neared the square, he almost ran a stoplight when he noticed Paige a half a block away, hand-in-hand with a little girl walking into a white brick building. He rounded the square, almost mechanically, then drove into a parking space thirty yards from the front entry where a monument identifying the Camden Grove Public Library sat in a small bed of flowers.

His curiosity, his need to see Emmie for himself, pricked at him like a splinter against his skin and wouldn't let him rest. Putting reason to the wind, he got out of the Jeep, walked the distance to the library door, and entered before his conscience or fear itself talked him out of it.

The scent that accompanies books, like traces of history married to ink, surrounded him as he stepped inside. A wiry, little woman behind the circulation desk took little note of him as he scanned the tables and chairs at the entry and eased into the stacks, looking for Paige and Emmie. He had no plans to approach them, didn't have a plan at all, really. He just wanted to see them—both of them—together.

At the center of the main room, an easel chalkboard announcing Saturday Afternoon Story Hour flanked a decorative bale of hay. A cornucopia, devoid of fruit and vegetables but instead gushing a pile of board books, sat on top of the bale.

He could hear kids' voices toward the back and followed the sounds, staying to the right of the room behind the stacks, just out of sight.

Between shelves, he pulled some rarely used volume about the Portuguese culture from its perch and watched through the stacks as more moms and dads brought their kids to a large alphabet rug near the center of the room. He paged through the book thoughtlessly, his attention instead landing on the children congregating beyond the gap in the shelves.

The librarian directed the kids to take a seat on the letter at the beginning of their names. Maddox craned his neck to find the E.

When the noise finally settled and everyone had found a spot, there she sat, legs crisscrossed, on her letter. Her hair hung in brown, wispy ponytails tied with bright red bows. She wore a matching jacket and a smile that lit up the room—one that enhanced a dimple in her chin. A dimple like his.

He watched and listened as the librarian brought the crowd to attention with a gathering song. The children sang along as parents took seats and slowly meandered to the margins of the rug. As the short tune ended, the librarian held up a brightly colored book and asked if the children would like to hear a story about a tree and a boy who always took things from the tree but never gave back.

The kids clapped and squirmed around on their lettered spots.

Maddox was rapt, the pages he'd been absentmindedly turning now stilled. From his view, he could see her eyes, wide and attentive, her mouth slightly open, the tip of her tongue touching her lower lip. In that moment, he realized something. He'd never *really* looked at a person with Down syndrome before. He'd seen them at different times, but he now recognized, by the very act of watching Emmie, that in those instances before, he'd always looked away. As he watched her, something about the act of looking away now felt shameful.

The voice of the librarian. The words of the story as she read to the kids. The sight of a little girl sitting on her letter E. It all soaked into him with the same subtlety as the fragrance of the library. Like walking in, inhaling the spoors of some long-forgotten story, somehow had the makings to put him in a different place. One where limits were left at the door and ability—the kind most valued by society—wasn't held up as an idol. Where potential of another kind grew like a flower from a crack in the concrete.

And that little flower had a name.

Emmie.

Chapter Four

Paige

Paige counted Saturday Story Hour at the library as dedicated study time for herself, though since Maddox had shown up in town, she knew today's effort to focus would be weak at best.

She'd tossed and turned all night, trying to reconcile herself with the idea that Maddox had crossed over that line where a biological contributor became a personal stakeholder.

Long ago, she'd given up on his having any interest in her or their daughter. How was she supposed to process him suddenly showing up, claiming he knew nothing about Emmie?

Being single and protecting her daughter had been hard, yes, but she'd been in control of most of the variables. Now with Maddox in town, she didn't even know what the variables were, much less how to manage them.

After she settled Emmie on the carpet with the other kids, Paige retreated to her favorite study area, a small, glassed-in room within sight of the librarian and her Story Hour audience. From here, she could work undisturbed while Emmie remained occupied singing songs, listening to Ms. Bonn's readings, and doing the weekly craft. At least, that's the way it usually worked.

Just as she pulled a couple of books from her bag, the children on the other side of the glass closed out the last verse of their greeting song. She glanced up out of habit to see if Emmie was taking part. With lopsided ponytails swishing, her head bobbed with the rhythm of the tune.

Paige watched for a moment, wondering about Emmie, considering how she would react if she knew about Maddox.

When the song ended, she could hear the muffled excitement in Ms. Bonn's voice from beyond the glass as she held up a book to show to the children.

Out of guilt more than curiosity, Paige scanned the group to see how many parents had stayed to engage with their kids. A few occupied metal chairs circled around the alphabet rug. A couple more opted to sit on the floor closer to their children, and a small group of young, suburban-looking mothers sporting yoga pants and messy buns stood just beyond the children's area, likely exchanging recommendations on the juicy books they'd pulled from the romance section.

With a sigh, she dismissed her guilt and almost turned attention back to her own books when she caught sight of him standing behind the stacks, looking between shelves toward the kids.

Maddox.

For the second time in as many days, she couldn't breathe.

This time she saw *him* first, and something inside her stung.

Hurt.

Tingled.

She watched, paralyzed for a moment, almost as if she were sitting within sight of the boy from six years ago, the one who'd stolen away with what was left of her heart.

Finally, she swallowed the lump that choked off her air, pushed down the swell of anxiety rising in her core, and dropped her bag to the floor—the dead weight of it making a muted thud against the carpet.

Shoving herself from the chair, she swung open the glass door and took a circuitous route around the edge of the library, avoiding the pockets of patrons and parents. When she rounded the last row of stacks, there he stood, his profile enough to weaken her resolve and set her on edge. But that alone didn't douse her anger. In the seconds between seeing him and confronting him, what softened her was the sight of him wearing an expression of tenderness as he watched Emmie.

That's when her temper waned a little. Waned, but didn't evaporate altogether.

"What do you think you're doing here?" she hissed.

A couple of parents within the sound of her voice turned to look in their direction.

At first, Maddox stammered, "I-I was driving by and saw you from across the square. I—"

"You have no right to follow us around."

"I wasn't following you."

The parents, who ventured a second look, now began to whisper. Paige grabbed Maddox by the arm and pulled him away from the stacks. She didn't let go until they were both back in the study room, the door closed and facing each other. Weak-kneed, she sat down at the table, folding her arms to mask the shakiness.

Maddox slipped into the seat across from her, shielding her from the view of the curious parents. "Look, Paige, you're right. Maybe I shouldn't have come in. I just wanted to—"

"To what, Maddox? See Emmie? Well, now you've seen her, so you can go back to your life and leave us to ours. We were doing fine before you showed up."

"That's good. I mean, I'm glad you're doing okay."

"Why did you even come to Camden Grove? Why now?"

He looked away, as if trying to find words. "That's what I was trying to tell you yesterday." Raising his eyes to meet hers, he continued. "Before three months ago, I didn't even know there was an Emmie. I thought you'd long forgotten about me when the letters stopped. And then there were other things—"

"I wrote constantly," she cut in. "For months, but you never wrote back."

"I know. At least, I do now. My mother gave me some of those letters—all of them she could save—three months ago." He looked away. "And I guess that answers my question about whether you got any of *my* letters."

For a moment, Paige sat numb at the aftershock. "I don't understand."

He looked as if he were trying to summon the right words. "After I left for boot camp, everything changed. You remember my father." It wasn't a question, so he didn't wait for an answer. "My enlistment became his obsession. Everything about it was strategically planned and put in place: boot camp, my CO's, my assignments. I thought it was made that way on purpose, to harden the Colonel's son since I didn't follow his original plan and attend the Marine Corps University."

"You'll understand if I don't exactly bowl over with sympathy." She meant her sarcasm to bite, but it came out weak.

"He waylaid our letters, Paige, threw them away. Mom said he thought I'd change course if I knew what'd happened with you. When she figured out he was throwing away your letters, she'd pull them from the trash when he left the house. Who knows what happened to mine. I'm sure he had some connection with somebody in postal detail."

His expression was earnest, but Paige tried to dismiss it.

"I wish I'd never asked you to send your letters through him. If he hadn't convinced me it would be best that way—"

"Your mom could've said something." She cut him off. "She made a decision, too. One that wasn't hers to make."

He bowed his head. "I'm not defending what she did, far from it. I'm still trying to understand it myself. It boils down to him. She lived with a commanding officer for a long time. He didn't leave that disposition at base. It came home with him every day, even after he retired."

"But you bought it, Maddox. You believed I didn't write to you when I promised I would."

"I asked. For weeks, I looked for letters. Asked my parents if they'd heard from you when they came to boot camp graduation. But they told me . . . that you'd moved on, and so should I."

"How convenient!" she snapped.

"I know it wasn't right, and no matter how much I want to do something about that, I can't now. All I can do is—"

"Show up and become a dad all of a sudden?"

"No." He stopped and stared into her eyes, clearly not knowing what he truly wanted. He turned away, looked through the glass at Emmie. A moment passed. "She's got the same color hair as you."

"Don't patronize me by side-stepping the elephant in the room. She has Down syndrome, Maddox. How would your father feel about that?" She coughed out a humorless laugh. "I'm sure that would've thrown a wrench in his plan, having me, a second-rate screw-up, around *and* a granddaughter with special needs?"

"I'm not patronizing you, Paige." He faced her. "I'll admit, finding out about Emmie and the . . . circumstances . . . If I'm honest, that's . . . a lot, but," he paused, "maybe I could meet her."

"No." The answer slipped out like it had been sliced clean from the air. "She won't be a part of your half-cocked effort to make yourself somehow feel a little more responsible because you drove a few miles to say hello to your poor, challenged idea of a mistake."

Paige spat out the words as if they tasted like gasoline on her tongue. "I'll not let you dip your toe in to see how it feels, then watch you pull it out when the water's too cold for comfort. Emmie doesn't deserve that, and neither do I." She leaned forward. "In fact, why don't you go back home to *the Colonel* and tell him all about his granddaughter. How she's *afflicted* with an extra chromosome, and he doesn't have to worry about you becoming involved. But don't share the little tidbit that what he would see as a biological mishap just happens to make her the most amazing human being on the planet. I really wouldn't want him to realize how much he's missed out on just because he's a world-class jerk." With the final sharp syllable, she leaned back in her seat. "Yeah, seems there's been plenty of secret-keeping. Think I'll keep that little nugget to myself."

Immediately, she felt the nastiness of her words fall like a heavy curtain on her chest as their effect bore out in Maddox's expression. For so long, her emotions had been a coiled-up viper with a store of venom waiting for a place to strike. But now that she'd found her target, she hadn't been liberated at all. She felt sick.

Finally, Maddox spoke. "I won't be able to tell him. He's dead."

The weight of his words and the subdued way he delivered them underscored her harshness. Somewhere, in the middle of the anger, awkwardness, and embarrassment, she felt smothered. With a trembling hand to her forehead, she propped her elbow on the table but couldn't bring herself to apologize. "You should go."

"I never wanted to hurt you, Paige." He eased from his seat, but instead of turning to leave, he looked her in the eye as if he were waiting to say something he couldn't force out. After another second's pause, he reached for a pen on the table and scribbled his cell number on a page of her notepad. "I'll be in town a few more days. If I can do . . . anything." His voice trailed off.

When the muffled sound of children clapping broke the silence, he turned toward the glass door and left.

Chapter Five

Maddox

The walk back to his Jeep left Maddox heavy with feelings too deeply buried to name. As it looked, a few more days in Camden Grove wouldn't likely make any difference. Paige had made pretty clear she had no intention of another visit or letting Emmie see him, and that left him no closer to a solution.

He had a daughter. Too many times in too many countries, he had seen enlisted men leave behind women after completed tours—bellies swollen in consequence of some one-nighter—never to see them again, never to man up to their responsibilities. And though he had to admit, the prospect of not coming to Camden Grove at all had crossed his mind, it wasn't because he wanted to snub his obligations, financial or otherwise.

The real wrestle had been more complex than that. It was a combination of things, not the least of which was upsetting any kind of balance that, surely by now, Paige must have found and that he had found, too, until the bombshell his mother dropped.

His loyalty to his team played into the equation just as much. He'd made a commitment years ago—one that had settled into his bones and found a home in his blood. That and, more significantly, something inside him confirmed that seeing Paige again had the potential to throw everything into a tailspin for all of them.

Finally, though, his conscience, over three long months, troubled him until he admitted to himself that he couldn't be that man, the one to leave behind a child, no matter how long it had been or how much would shift.

As the afternoon saw the sun tilt further to the west, he wasn't ready to return to the bed-and-breakfast. Personable as the Mulligans were, he had no desire to chat about those things they found of interest.

Instead, he sat parked on the fountain side of the town square and eventually moved to a weathered bench, watching the water bubble up from the boat-shaped fount and trickle back to its origin. He spent more than an hour there, forcing himself not to look continuously toward the library end of the square. Hoping that Paige might drive by on her way home, he thought maybe just one more glimpse of the both of them would offer a prompting one way or another about whether he should occupy his next hour with packing and leaving or settling in for another couple of days.

He was right. A short five minutes later, she passed the square in a blue compact Nissan. Two red bows visible from the back seat and a fleeting glimpse of Paige driving behind sunglasses did nothing to settle the matter.

After she'd driven out of sight, he listened to the whispering sounds of the water, hoping they'd give him an answer. Finally, he stood and tossed in a coin without a wish, climbed back into the Jeep, and headed toward the Mulligans'.

Halfway to the other end of town, with the Jeep's tank nearly empty, Maddox pulled into one of only two filling stations he'd seen since his arrival. A slipshod congregation of high school students had gathered along the parking lot's edge, among them the truck and owner he'd become acquainted with the first day at the ice cream shop. Quarterback and a group of new friends—different kids, this time—sat with their feet swinging from the tailgate of an adjacent pickup, their laughter echoing across the lot above the heavy bass thumping from speakers in the truck bed.

As Maddox parked the Jeep at an empty pump, he nodded toward the familiar stares of the jock whose feet had stopped swinging. The kid turned away and took a swig from an amber bottle, then burst into laughter again, giving no more than a second glance to Maddox.

After paying for his fuel and a few snacks, he hit the release button on the dash, opened the fuel door, and began to fill up. The numbers sluggishly clicked on the old-style pump, and he wondered how many other things in this town were ancient but still functional.

Instead of waiting aimlessly, he secured the nozzle and stepped over the hose in search of something to wash his windshield. Someone had placed an orange five-gallon bucket with dirty water beside the pump. The handle of a submerged squeegee lay against the bucket just above the murky water, and when he reached for it, his hand met hers.

Just as surprised as she appeared to be, neither of them spoke at first. She must've pulled up while he was inside. Paige quickly withdrew her hand and glanced over her shoulder, back toward the car on the other side of the pump. His eyes trailed hers toward the ponytails with the bright red bows visible just above the car's window frame.

"I didn't follow you this time." He smiled, then without thinking, added, "Did you follow me?"

The shock on her face deepened. "Are you crazy?" She looked over her shoulder again.

Then he took the squeegee from the bucket and walked toward her car.

"What are you doing?"

"I'm washing your windshield."

"I can do that myself." She followed him around the pump. Before they reached her car, Paige blocked his way. She lowered her voice. "I said I've got it. Emmie's in the car, and I don't want her to see you."

"Why? Does she know who I am?"

"No," Paige hissed, lowering her voice. "I haven't told her anything about you."

"Then you shouldn't worry. I'm not going to mess anything up just by washing your window."

"You have no clue the effect it could have for her to get even an inkling of an idea about who you are."

"Paige—" he stopped long enough to look deeply into her eyes "—when I saw her at the library, she was beautiful, and I didn't even get to see her up close. I just want to see her face. I promise I won't do another thing unless you say it's okay."

"Then will you leave us alone?"

"Is that what you really want?"

"Mommy?" the little girl's muffled voice called from inside the car.

Paige turned around. "What, honey?"

"I'm thirsty."

Paige looked back at him, and after hesitating, she nodded toward the windshield. He stepped up to her car with the squeegee dripping at his side and ran it slowly across the glass as she opened the rear door.

He could see through ribbons of water, Emmie raising a no-spill cup to drink. With quick glances between strokes, he watched as Paige took the cup and settled the little girl with her library book. When she finished, she closed the door, pulled the gas nozzle from the car, and shoved it back in its cradle. "That's good enough." She glanced at the window.

"I didn't clean the other side."

Without another word, Paige got in the car, started the engine, and pulled away.

Maddox stood by the pump, watching the car drive toward the street. He could see Emmie stretching to look out the window. When she saw him, she smiled and waved. That was the moment he knew he couldn't leave Camden Grove just yet.

Chapter Six

Paige

Saturday night. Sunday. Sunday night. The hours all blurred into a string of emotional arguments Paige had with herself. For every time Emmie walked into the room or they sat at a meal together or she tucked her little girl into bed, images of Maddox came to mind. Not just the thoughts she'd conjured up so many times before of a deadbeat father with no heart—if only she could be so focused—and not even pictures in her head of the way things used to be.

What she more often saw was the twinge in his expression when she'd lashed out at him at the library. Her words had cut to the quick. When she tried to empty her thoughts of the hurt in his eyes, the only image that took its place was when she saw him peeking over volumes of reference books, looking at Emmie with a smile on his face. A genuine smile. Or she'd imagine him cleaning her windshield just to see her again.

By Sunday night, she was so exhausted that sleep came, but it wasn't peaceful. In fact, fitful dreams replaced a restless reality.

In the dreams, they were under a tree, she and Maddox. The same one from years ago where he first approached her, when she suspected she was the butt of someone's mean-spirited joke. She couldn't fathom what a decent-looking guy with any kind of social status might possibly want with her.

Bitterness rose in her dreams like a fog climbing out of a steamy field. Then she spoke to him, under the influence of sleep's convoluted timing, telling him defiantly that she was pregnant. And she waited. Waited for him to run, but he didn't move. Why couldn't she get him to move? Hadn't he heard her?

In the same dream-induced passage of time, she looked down and found a tiny baby Emmie wrapped in a hospital blanket in her arms. She dared to look again into his eyes, knowing her baby had Down syndrome, knowing he would surely leave then.

Still, he didn't move.

Anger swelled inside her. She *wanted* him to leave. She could do this alone. Wasn't it better to stake that claim now than bear the heartache of being left? Again?

When he didn't move, she fought with arms now empty, her fingers digging into the cotton of his shirt, wrapped and knotted in cloth, willing it to tear, to rip away the hurt.

Moments later, when she thrashed herself awake, the darkness of the early morning still sat on the windowsill, and her arms lay drained, tangled in the cool sheets.

The house was quiet. Her hand, finally free of the linens, found its way to her stomach to touch the skin side of her empty womb. Thoughts of the dream lingered until she crawled out of bed.

The nightlight in the hall—an elephant with its trunk holding the bulb—lit her path into the kitchen. She pulled a quart-sized carton of orange juice from the refrigerator and turned it up where she stood. Never had she allowed Emmie to do that, but sometimes being a parent came with privileges worth abusing, if only out of sight of the child.

After returning the carton, she trudged to the hall closet and pulled out a lap blanket. Sleep was a lost hope now, and she knew it. Curled up on the couch, Paige drew her feet beneath her and draped the blanket over her shoulders.

Did she dare even think it?

Emmie was his daughter, too.

When the office opened a few hours later, Paige sat at her desk, bleary-eyed, the muttering to herself turning into a full-fledged battle.

"Sounds like a fascinating conversation."

Paige dropped the pen she held and turned to Ava. Her doctor friend had been someone she'd trusted but hesitated to confide in, only because she didn't open her heart to anyone, really. If there were a trustworthy soul, though, she'd found that quality in Ava.

Paige consciously closed her open mouth.

"Sorry, I didn't mean to interrupt," Ava smiled. "What's going on?"

"Oh, nothing."

"Don't ever try to snooker your way out of a parking ticket with a lie. You're not very good at it."

Rolling her chair to the desk, Paige snatched the pen from the floor and threw it into an open drawer.

"Want to talk about it?" Ava cocked her head.

She shrugged.

"It's nothing here at the office, is it?"

"No, of course not. This office, moving to Camden Grove with Emmie, getting to be friends with you and the girls—that's all been my saving grace these past few months."

"Emmie okay?"

"It's not Emmie. At least . . . not yet."

Ava circled the counter and sat in the chair across from Paige, her expression laced with concern. "I've got a few minutes before my first appointment. Why don't you tell me what's bothering you?"

Paige hesitated. "You know when you came to Nashville and found me in that dive of an apartment with Emmie?"

Only months ago, Ava had located Paige to ask for help in indicting their mutual former creep of an employer for insurance fraud. It had been a huge fiasco that somehow turned out better than Paige or Ava either one could have dreamed.

"There are a lot of things I'd rather not remember about Nashville, and finding you two in that apartment building ranks at the top of the list."

"You know what I told you about being all alone?"

"Best I remember, you said that after you got pregnant, your family kicked you out and that Emmie's father wasn't a very supportive party either."

"Yes, and all that's true, or . . . at least I *thought* all of it was true."

"I'm not following."

Paige fidgeted with a paper clip. "On Friday, after everybody left the office, I was getting ready to go home. . . ."

"Yes?"

"Just as I was finishing up, someone came in the front door."

"Aaand?"

She looked at Ava. "It was Emmie's father."

"Oh, I see. Wow . . . and what did he have to say?"

"He wanted to talk. I told him he could wait like I did all those years. But he asked about Emmie."

"Did he threaten you?" Ava's turned solemn.

"No. He just wanted to talk."

"So, did you talk?"

"No, not then anyway." Paige twisted the paper clip until it broke.

"Did you see him over the weekend?"

"As a matter of fact, I did run into him on Saturday . . . a couple of times, not intentionally, but we met nonetheless."

"And how did that turn out?"

"I don't know. A disaster?" She shrugged. "Ava, he told me he'd just found out about Emmie three months ago."

"Wait, I thought he didn't want anything to do with her when he discovered you were pregnant."

"That's just it. I thought that because he never responded to my letters, but now he's telling me he never knew."

"I don't understand."

Paige took a deep breath. "When we graduated from high school, Maddox had plans for the Marines. Or rather, his dad, this high-scale officer, expected him to go to the Marine Corps

University. He ended up in the Marines. But as an enlistee rather than going the university route. We were both pretty miserable at the thought of him leaving, or so I thought. I mean, I knew he wanted to enlist, but I still felt like he loved me enough to regret going." She shifted in her chair.

"Anyway, we had an arrangement where I was supposed to keep in touch with him through his dad until boot camp was over. The Colonel said he thought it would be best that way because Maddox was an officer's son. If he got too much mail during boot camp, they would target him as some kind of military pansy, and that wouldn't do. Anyway, the night before he left? Well, that's when Emmie was conceived."

Understanding seeped into Ava's expression. "So, you wrote to Maddox, told him about your pregnancy, but the Colonel never passed those letters on."

"Every day for months, I wrote. Then I finally stopped. I thought he'd dropped us until three days ago. That's when he told me he never knew. And, yes, his father had kept my letters from him and must've detoured Maddox's letters to me. I guess the Colonel saw me as too much of a distraction from what he'd mapped out for his son."

"A Colonel?" Ava's eyebrows raised. "Maddox had some pretty stiff pressure, then. So how did he find out?"

"His father died some time back, but his mother had kept the letters. She gave them to him. I guess after her conscience got the better of her."

"So, where does that leave you and Emmie?"

"I don't know. That's just it." She put a hand to her head. "I've been battling with this all weekend, Ava. I don't know if I'm ready for this guy Emmie's never met to suddenly walk into our lives as her father." Her eyes brimmed with tears. "We were just getting settled here in Camden Grove, finding our way, and this happens."

"Is that it?"

"What do you mean?

"Is that *all* you're upset about?"

Paige twisted the broken paper clip feverishly. "I'm still angry that he didn't come back before now, didn't have more faith in me than taking his parents' word for it. Mad that *I* thought we had something more than *he* did." Her voice rose with every word.

"You said you don't know if you're ready. Will you ever be?"

She slumped, forehead in hand. "What do you think I should do?"

"Did he say how long he's planning to be here?"

"No." She shrugged. "He's still enlisted, so I'm sure he has to go back sometime soon."

The front door opened, and Mrs. Griggs, a woman in her sixties with a fondness for splashy colors and one too many pieces of jewelry, took a seat in the waiting room.

Paige glanced at the patient. "Look, I know you have to get to work, and you're back-to-back all day. I'll just have to figure this out myself."

Ava touched Paige's hand, still fidgeting with a piece of the paper clip. She lowered her voice. "You're used to doing things alone, but, just so you know, going solo on everything isn't something you have to do anymore. You've got friends here." She tapped the desk. "And I've got an idea. Why don't you let Emmie go with Logan and Toby this afternoon? They're fishing with Wyatt and his parents at the pond and then having a cook-out at the farm afterward."

Since becoming engaged to Logan, Ava had grown close to his parents, Margaret and Gus. They and his twin brother, Wyatt, along with Wyatt's wife, Lydia, had all been frequent stop-ins at the office, adopting Paige and Emmie into their circle as if they were family.

Before she could respond, Ava continued. "Carly, Jessie, and Lydia are coming to my place to talk over a few wedding details. You could come help us. We could make it an all-out girls' night, and talk more then, if you're up for it."

Paige knew Carly would lighten the mood by telling stories of her latest photography escapades and her new guy from Chicago. She'd come to love Carly's carefree approach since they'd met a few months back. And though she'd just begun to get acquainted with Jessie, she knew to expect from her the same comical woes about being single she'd aired every other time they'd met. Get the two of them together, and they had a flair for perking up spirits.

Maybe she *could* use a minute to herself with some girlfriends. She slowly nodded. "That actually sounds like exactly what I need."

"Just to ice the cake, I'm making homemade tortilla chips to go with some salsa Margaret canned this summer and gave to me." Ava winked.

Logan's mother's salsa had been a treat at the office grand opening back in July, and it was enough of a nudge to seal the deal.

"I'll call Logan at lunch and tell him you'll drop Emmie off this evening. Let's say at six?"

"Six," Paige repeated.

Ava stepped to the waiting room, called in Mrs. Griggs, and held the door open for her first patient of the day. The jingling from the older woman's bangle bracelets sang her arrival all the way down the hall.

Chapter Seven

Maddox

That Monday morning, Maddox bathed in the claw-foot Victorian tub of his adjoining blue bathroom. He was used to showers, and plenty of times, during some remote deployment, he had cleaned up the best he could with a damp cloth and bottle of water. This, odd as it was, seemed like an undeserved luxury—less customary than cold military showers but more cleansing than a water bottle. The occasion found him soaking for the third time since arriving at the Mulligans' in a deep and steaming tub filled to the rim, easing the tension in his shoulders built up over the last few months.

Since he'd been in Camden Grove, living in a blue room, there'd been no shortage of time to himself to think, and now he sat in the tub, thinking again. He'd waited all weekend, hoping for word from Paige. In the end, he knew it was too much to expect.

Beside the tub, Glenna had stocked a small table with a couple of towels and washcloths. On top, he'd emptied his pockets of the

Jeep key, his wallet, the good luck charm he always carried, and the worn photo he'd taken six years ago of Paige and him at the boathouse—the one he'd shown the girl at the Creamery.

Paige smiled with her eyes in that picture. That had been the same compliment he'd paid her the day she'd given him the good luck charm. And her sandy brown hair, backlit by the cabin light inside the boat, gave her an angelic-looking glow, as hard-earned as any *true* angel's, he thought.

He reached over the towels, water streaming from his hand, and picked up the buckeye. Lucky or not, it had reminded him of her and the moment he fell in love—the reason he'd kept it all these years. He wondered if there was room for those kinds of feelings anymore. Room in her heart *or* his. He'd never given much credence to a tree seed being a good luck charm, but if it were, he doubted this little misshapen buckeye had a shred of luck left in it.

Turning it over in water-wrinkled fingers, he thought about the day she'd given it to him.

After his father's retirement, Maddox's mother, Bonnie, had wanted to move somewhere away from the military scene, though everyone knew the Colonel's foot would always stay planted firmly with his comrades and connections. At Bonnie's request, they'd ended up in Music City, a place she'd always wanted to go. Letting her choose their landing spot for retirement was one of the few concessions the Colonel had ever made for his wife. She'd followed him for thirty years, but that meant very little in the long and short of it.

Once boredom set in, he'd uproot them again. The military way of life never dies that easily, so the Nashville suburb of Treemont was a stop-off, at best.

Maddox had liked the new move well enough. The neighborhood was nice. School was good. Though he was athletic, he hadn't arrived before any of the fall sports sign-ups, but he didn't really mind. He at least had the benefit of being one of those guys who fit in wherever he went—a perk that had given him a reason to hang out after school and stay away from home a little longer.

The Colonel's need to authorize his every step, compounded by the man's restlessness with retirement, left Maddox searching for reasons to get home later. By the afternoons, the Colonel had already been up thirteen hours, had run through all the daily routines with his wife, and had enough energy left over to make any number of regimented demands on his son.

The closer he got to graduation, the more Maddox felt like a recruit in his own home, and though he looked forward to enlistment only a few months away, it got old having a commanding officer at the dinner table instead of a dad. At least before long, he'd be enlisted for real. The part of that scenario he dreaded most was telling the Colonel that he'd chosen standard enlistment over enrollment in the Marine Corps University. It would be a fight.

The day he first noticed Paige, he hadn't found any good excuse to stay after school. He had exited the main building just behind her, and though he didn't realize it then, he soon found out she lived in the subdivision just before his.

As he followed, watching her walk just ahead, he had become absorbed in the way she seemed content being alone. While others left school headed to the mall in a whirlwind of small herds and cliques, she sauntered along by herself, taking in sights, sounds, and smells, like the outdoors was her own little Shangri-La.

The fall leaves had been turning, much like they were now in Camden Grove. Halfway home, he'd watched as Paige veered from the sidewalk toward a large tree with leaves the color of salmon. It grew in a stretch of grass just beyond a plot of manicured hedges.

At the bulging roots of the tree, she sat down and began gathering something from the ground. The first day, he passed on by, satisfied to leave her to her interests, but by the fourth, his curiosity got the better of him.

On that day, after Paige took her place under the tree, Maddox paused to watch her for a bit, then crossed the grass toward her. She never glanced his way as he approached, choosing instead to keep her head down, either engrossed in what she was doing or unconcerned about seeming unsociable.

"Hey," Maddox finally spoke.

She looked up with squinted eyes. "Yeah?"

"I'm Maddox." He nodded back toward the walkway. "I've followed you home a few days this week."

"You a stalker?"

His brow stitched together in objection. "No. I live in Harvest Crest just past your subdivision, and I guess my last class is farther from the school's exit door than yours."

She nodded. "I'm Paige." At first, she hesitated, but then she gestured toward the ground with a nod. "Well, you want to sit?"

Unlike most of the other girls at Treemont High, this one seemed to have no preference if he stayed or went. Unused to a lack of schoolgirl enthusiasm, he was drawn to join her as much out of curiosity as the fact that Paige was attractive in a natural kind of way.

She had none of the traits girls at school would call beautiful. Her hair was cropped in a short, sandy-brown bob— no artificial highlights or bold colors, just sun-streaked and straight. And her eyes weren't what anybody would call striking. They were blue. Not baby or Nordic or electric blue. More gunmetal. Subtle.

Her poreless complexion, though, was creamy and velvet, without a line or blemish. Even when she squinted, the edges along her eyes seemed to groove instead of crease.

Taking a place on the grass in front of her, he looked down at her lap. In the folds of a sweater draped over her legs lay a small pile of spiny, yellow-green seedpods like a school of pufferfish caught in a net. "What's that you're doing?"

"You wouldn't understand." She leaned back on her hands.

He mimicked her movement and tilted back himself. "Try me."

"Okay." She raised her eyebrows as if to challenge him. "I'm shelling buckeyes."

"Buckeyes?"

"Yeah." Her voice came out snappy. "Ever heard of 'em?"

"Of course, I have. Ohio State. Their football team's pretty good this year." He snickered.

"Like I said." She went back to peeling at the seedpods.

"So, I give. Why are you shelling buckeyes?"

She cocked her head. "Because they're poison, and I'm premeditating a murder."

At first, Maddox stuttered, "Y-you're what?"

She rolled her eyes and huffed out a half-laugh as if she were sloughing off the stupid that had just settled like a mist around her.

"I'm collecting them. You know, good luck charms?"

"Buckeyes are good luck charms?"

"'S what some people believe." She tugged at another pod.

He picked up an unopened shell from the ground beside him and turned it over in his hand, then pointed to her loaded sweater. "You must need a lot of luck."

"I'll take all I can get," she said and tossed a pod to the ground. "If you really want to know, I'm selling them."

Though it seemed weird, Maddox responded without a flinch. "Where do you sell buckeyes?"

"Ohio."

He snickered again, not knowing yet whether to believe her. "Don't you think that's kind of ambitious, selling buckeyes to people in Ohio? Kind of like selling milk to a cow. Isn't that like their state tree or something?"

Paige ignored his jibe. "There's a shortage."

"Whatever you say." He rolled the plump shell from finger to finger. "Need some help?"

"Suit yourself."

He grabbed a handful from her lap, leaned against the tree, and began peeling. They sat quietly for a few minutes. Then, Maddox broke the silence. "So how is it that Ohio has a shortage of buckeyes?"

Paige inhaled, then let it go. "Not Ohio. *Anker Valley*, Ohio. Turns out the gaming commission there put out an ad to draw people into their casino, saying they were handing out lucky buckeyes. Some old guy on an oxygen tank took the very first one from the dish, put it in his left back pocket, and ended up walking out with twenty-five thousand dollars. Since some big-time columnist picked up the story, they've now got a demand, but guess what?"

"A lack of buckeyes?"

Paige gave a curt nod.

"And how did you find out about the deficit of a bunch of overgrown acorns in Anker Valley, Ohio, when you're all the way down here in Tennessee?"

She pinched her lips together and tore more forcefully at a shell. "My dad's a gambler. He likes to make trips up there with a buddy to the casino. One of his old fraternity brothers runs it." She brushed a falling pod from her lap.

"Last month, they went for a big poker tournament. When he came home with two-thousand fewer dollars in his pocket, he told my mom the whole story about the old man on the oxygen tank and the buckeye gimmick, trying to convince her that this casino was the luckiest place in the world and that, on the next trip, he was bound to win back his losses and then some."

"So why don't you give them to your dad? Sounds like he needs the luck."

"Not a chance." She grimaced. "The way I see it, odds are always stacked against gamblers. They're just too blind, addicted, or stupid to see it."

"So," Maddox wondered aloud, "you're sending them with him to sell to the blind, addicted, and stupid?"

She grinned. "No, my dad's not a part of this business deal. He'd just blow the money at the slots. I made a call to the frat brother. He says he'll pay me a dollar apiece if I send him a bulk shipment. FedEx is a little more reliable."

"A buck a buckeye. That's probably the craziest business venture I've ever heard of."

"Yeah, well, you can call it crazy; you can say it's dumb; I don't even care if you laugh, 'cause between the tree in our backyard, this one, and those in Richland Park, I stand to make a thousand bucks for a few hours' work."

Maddox raised his eyebrows. "Not bad." He reached across her lap and turned up her hands. "Looks like you'll have earned it, though." Her fingers were red and scaly from the shelling.

She pulled them away and went back to work.

"So, what're you gonna do with all that money?"

She shrugged. "Hide it from my dad. Use it to leave home after graduation in a few months. College."

"Don't you think there's a better way than picking up tree seeds?"

"Probably, but I don't have a car to drive myself to a job; my parents aren't exactly supportive; and neighborhood babysitting money goes only so far. So, if you have any bright ideas for me to make cash, I'm all ears." She looked at him, eyebrows raised.

"I'm joining the Marines. They pay your way."

"Congratulations. The military is not the kind of life I want."

"Why not?" He tossed a peeled buckeye in her lap.

"Because I like to know where I'm going, not leave it to somebody else to decide."

"But there are all kinds of other options if you look in the right places."

"I'm sure there are—" she held up a buckeye "—but until I find them, guess I'll just have to take advantage of the money growing on trees around here."

"Touché." Maddox smiled. "Don't guess I've ever thought about channeling my inner Pocahontas enough to harvest buckeyes, though."

Paige shot him a sharp look. "Are you making fun of me?"

After a few drawn-out seconds of a staring match, the grooves in her face twitched and deepened, and they both burst into laughter.

When the laughing died, Maddox leaned forward, wrapping his arms around his knees. "You smile with your eyes," he said.

She dropped her gaze. "I should get home now."

Maddox nodded. When they stood to leave, she loaded the shelled buckeyes into her backpack, having cleared all that had fallen on the ground.

"Want to walk home together tomorrow?" Maddox brushed stray pieces of seedpod from his pants.

She slowly agreed. "As long as your inner Pocahontas isn't involved."

"Deal." He grinned.

When he turned to leave, Paige called from behind, "Hey . . . Maddox." He looked back.

She tossed him a buckeye. The dark-brown, nut-like seed, shiny and more flat than the others they'd shelled, looked like a small flying saucer. And without the light brown mark that made it resemble the eye of a deer.

"What's this for?"

"It doesn't have the lighter spot on it, and that's what gamblers rub for luck."

"So, you gave me a reject?"

"No, I was saving it, 'cause it's the most unique buckeye I've gotten from this whole tree. My theory is, because it's one of a kind, it'll bring more luck than any of them."

"Then I guess I'll carry it with me forever."

"Alright then." She nodded, smiled, and turned for home.

"Good morning, young man." Glenna lay a ringed linen napkin on a plate as Maddox entered the dining room to a table spread with exactly three place settings. For the third day in a row, patterned china, crystal glasses, and polished silverware made up the breakfast table. His hosts had spared nothing. They'd already set out gravy boats and a basket of biscuits, a plate of sausages and bacon, eggs, fruit, strawberry preserves, and a freshly filled butter dish. The breakfast smells had tantalized him all the way upstairs.

In an effort to make small talk, Maddox nodded toward the table. "With a meal like this, I'm surprised I could get a room with you this weekend."

"Oh, we have people trickle in and out." Glenna smiled. "The most traffic comes during the community festival when the town comes alive and Kane Wiggs, over at the barbecue place, hosts the luau. We're busy as bees then."

Hugh pulled out a chair for his wife. "We like it best when there's just one or two, we do." He gestured for Maddox to sit, then joined them at the head of the table.

"Keeps things nice and cozy," Glenna added.

Maddox again eyed the table spread with steaming food. The dish sets had been different every day, all antique patterns, gold-rimmed and flowered. "You don't have to use all your good dishes for me. I'm used to mess hall trays and meals from a mylar bag."

Glenna dismissively waved. "Nonsense, honey. You're our guest. It's how we do things around here. Only the best."

Once they were all seated, Glenna offered her customary blessing on the food, and the three began passing each other serving dishes.

Hugh opened the conversation. "So, here to visit a friend, but ye haven't been out for more than a mite since ye got here."

"Hugh," Glenna scolded, gentle as a honey-drip. "That's not our business."

Maddox grinned and raised his glass of juice for a drink, amused at the old man's prod.

Glenna, with a Cheshire smile, spread a generous dollop of butter onto a steaming biscuit. "It must be a lady friend."

Hugh rolled his eyes.

"Um, it is."

"Well, what're ye waiting for, lad? She'll shrivel up at this pace."

Glenna patted Hugh's hand. "Not everybody goes at the same clip as you do. I'm sure he has his reasons." She turned to Maddox. "What's her name, dear?"

At first, he paused. Something about the way Glenna touched Hugh's hand, the way the two balanced each other, caught him off-guard. Could've been that the hours he'd stayed to himself in the Blue Room had fueled the need to share. Or maybe being in the company of strangers he'd likely never meet again broke his resolve. Whatever the case, he opened up. "Her name's Paige. I stopped by to see her Friday when I came into town. I wanted to talk, . . . but she didn't."

He sawed at a piece of sausage with his knife, letting more of his thoughts come out than he'd planned. "We knew each other back in high school a few years ago, but I moved away."

Glenna and Hugh sat quietly and listened as Maddox focused on his plate.

"Before we met, I already had plans to go into the Marines. My dad was a Marine, my granddad, and his dad before him." He poked at his food. "It's in the Granger blood, they always said."

Hugh's bushy brows drew close together. "Is it in yours?"

Maddox nodded, his head bowed toward his plate. "The Marines has been a good place for me."

"What happened to Paige?" Glenna dribbled gravy from the China boat over another biscuit.

"When I left, things more or less dissolved."

She smiled. "And now, here you are. Oh, I just adore second chances."

Maddox shook his head. "I don't think that's what we're talking about here, Miz Glenna."

"Well, honey, you've got to try to visit with your friend again. No doubt she just needs a little time to warm up to the idea."

"Maybe." Maddox sighed. "I told her I would give her some room, but I don't much expect to see her before I leave to go back to base."

"That's your first mistake, darlin'." Glenna shook her head. "You can't be passive, especially when it comes to us women."

Hugh's fork scraped against his plate. "There's something to be said for a man keeping his word, there is."

"No need for him to go back on his word." Glenna cocked her head. "There are ways to work around that. Does she work somewhere?"

"Yes, ma'am." He said. "She works at the clinic in town. That's where I went to see her on Friday."

"That new doctor's office down on Brewster? Why, I've been meaning to go have my triglycerides tested there ever since that office opened." Glenna gathered her plate and glass, having barely eaten. "You and Hugh finish up your breakfast. Then, why don't you come out back to the garden? I think we can muster up a plan for you to keep your promise and connect with this girl all at the same time."

Maddox watched Glenna disappear toward the kitchen, wondering what she was thinking, sensing that maybe he should have kept quiet.

With the passing of the weekend, he'd forgotten about the Mulligans' earlier invitation to visit the conservatory and garden. The high hedgerow between his bedroom window and the backyard hid the view, except for the top of a towering oak, so he had no idea what he was missing.

Just beyond an unassuming breakfast nook, he followed Hugh around the corner to the room that the Mulligans hadn't included on their initial tour.

The octagon-shaped conservatory seemed almost other-worldly, each of the angles of glass segmenting the room in perfect increments. At the base of each segment, large plants of different varieties bloomed as if from the glazed tile floor.

The vaulted glass ceiling, framed with massive oak beams, allowed the sunlight, rising above the east side of the garden's hedgerow, to light the room. From the pinnacle of the dome hung an antique brass lantern with a large metal chain, links the size of a man's fist.

Maddox walked around a circular table beneath the hanging lantern. As he absorbed the light that spilled into the room, he heard Hugh's voice already beyond the glass outside.

Glenna waved from the garden and pointed to the only segmented pane with a door. "Come through right there."

When he stepped from the conservatory onto the stone path, he finally realized the magnitude of the garden. Space, color, architecture, and landscape all came together in perfect order.

Surrounded by hedges on three sides, the evergreen wall met the house in a natural enclosure. In the center of the garden, likely two hundred paces away, stood a massive live oak tree, skirted with lush ferns, limbs hanging down like a doting grandmother.

From one of them, a rope swing dangled. Someone had notched the plank board wide enough to hold two people. The stone path wound around the oak to a pergola just beyond, still lush with bloomless climbing rose bushes holding on to the last of the warm weather.

Glenna and Hugh were right: it was a hidden piece of heaven.

"This is quite a garden."

Hugh bent to an open storage ottoman, where he retrieved a pair of scissors. "A beauty, yes. And it brings us pleasure, but preparing it for winter's quite a job."

"Is there anything I can do to help?"

"Oh, honey, we have work to do, but it's not the kind you're thinking about." She slipped on a pair of garden gloves and turned to Hugh for the scissors. "I'll show Maddox around a little bit while you work on that bush, Hugh." She then laced a hand around Maddox's arm. "Let's take a walk around the path. I want to introduce you to my favorite things."

The rough steppingstones, laid in a mosaic along the mossy path, wound around the garden like yarn dropped in a slack string before being knitted. Once they'd reached the far side of the oak, she took him to one of the garden's sunny nooks. On the ground, mounted on a rustic platform, lay a large copper plate the size of a bass drum. "Have you ever seen one of these?"

Maddox nodded. "Yes, ma'am. I've seen a sundial before, but this one is a little different."

"That's because it's a perpetual sundial and calendar. I can always come out here and know exactly what time of day and year it is just by looking at that sundial. I've waited here sometimes just to see if I could watch time passing."

Glenna turned to him and looked him straight in the eyes. "I've spent a lot of years watching shadows pass over that big slab of copper. Every time I come to this corner of the garden, it reminds me that, though I can't see it, my time is limited, and I can either work with it, or it may work against me." She tugged Maddox's arm and walked farther along the path, pointing out different plants and flowers, herbs, and ornamental trees, calling them by name.

"I don't have any illusion that you need to leave here with all the names of my backyard plants or a philosophical lesson on the passage of time. I do, however, believe you've met up with a unique challenge. And I think you just might benefit from a little botanical cultivation and a sensitivity to timing." Her voice dripped like a spoon dipped in molasses.

"I don't know that I follow you."

Glenna gently patted his arm again as they continued to walk. "Every flower, shrub, and herb in this garden is a symbol of something. Take roses, for example." She nodded to the thorny bushes climbing up the pergola. "They've done their time this year, but when they're in full bloom, they're just gorgeous. And every color means something: yellow says friendship; white means purity; pink, admiration; and red, passion. Flowers send messages. Seems to me you're in need of a timely message. Otherwise, how will your friend know she's worth your effort? If you don't show her any more energy than telling her to come to you when she's ready, she may question your sincerity, and we can't have that."

"But I just wanted to give her some space."

Glenna nodded. "Space is good to a point, but now it's time to charm her. That *is* what you want, isn't it?"

Maddox thought for a minute. "I don't know how either of us feels right now."

"Well, seems like you came an awful long way to be turned away." She paused. "And whether you know or not, you'll never be any closer to finding out unless you spend time with her. I think I can help you with that."

Maddox slowly grinned. "How's that?"

"I called Dr. Fenn's office while you were finishing breakfast and scheduled a check-up appointment. And wouldn't you know it? She so happened to have a cancellation this afternoon." She cupped her hand and whispered, "I keep that old Irishman around for luck, and it works sometimes." She chuckled.

Maddox's smile broadened. "I guess I should ask specifically how you plan to convince Paige to meet with me."

"I thought you'd never ask." Glenna led him on around the path at the turn farthest from the house. They arrived at the back hedge in the south corner of the yard. The backdrop of the evergreen barrier framed a massive flowering bush of blue blooming flowers. "We've had an unusual fall, warmest for as long as I can remember, just an extension of summer, really. Hugh's been draping a sheet over my hydrangeas during the cooler nights, so I'd have a few more weeks to enjoy them."

She fished her hand into the pocket of her yard apron, where she pulled out the scissors. "I want you to take these and cut some of those gorgeous blooms." She pulled a shoot close and snipped it at an angle. "Be sure to leave a good long stem, and I'll go get a vase for us to put them in."

"But—"

Glenna had already turned toward the house. "Cut maybe eight or ten, and don't forget some greenery. That just sets off a nice bouquet—the greenery." She was already back down the path before Maddox could say anything more.

When Glenna returned, she had a blue glass vase with a trumpeted neck. After she tucked and arranged the stems he'd cut and added the appropriate amount of greenery, she held the vase at arm's length to scrutinize her work. "Do you know why my hydrangeas are blue?"

He looked back at the towering bush with its enormous blooms. "No."

"Hydrangeas come in all kinds of colors from white to pink to blue with all shades of violet in between. A couple of years ago, that very plant was pastel pink." She shook her head. "Nature is a wonder, isn't it? I buried a bucket of rusty nails around that plant last fall, and this year, it came out vibrant blue."

Maddox kept quiet.

"Those rusty nails changed that bush but made it even more vivacious than before. Now, if I can do that with a bucket of rusty nails and a little bit of time, don't you think a vase of those flowers put in front of that girl could soften her heart at least a little?"

Maddox cocked his head and smirked.

She gathered the spare trimmings from the flowers and tucked them in her apron. "My appointment is at one o'clock. I'll put them right on her desk, and you'll never even have to break your promise to leave her to her own devices." She started back toward the house, calling over her shoulder. "You enjoy the garden and leave everything to me."

Maddox looked at the scissors in his hand, then bent one of the blue, lace-capped hydrangeas closer to inhale the scent, sweet and subtle. Just before she rounded the bend out of sight, he called out,

"Miz Glenna, you said every flower symbolizes something. What about hydrangeas?"

She turned and, with a big smile, cupped a hand round her mouth. "Forgiveness, darlin'. They mean forgiveness."

Chapter Eight

Paige

The office remained busy all morning with a steady flow of patients, office calls, and a visit from a drug rep who brought in lunch. Paige left her sandwich in the fridge and opted instead for the mushroom ravioli and chopped salad the rep provided from one of the Italian restaurants in Hartley. That was one perk of working in a doctor's office—always someone bringing in treats.

Until she could get additional help, Ava requested they stagger their lunches for the time being to cover any phone calls. She took eleven to noon, often leaving for a quick lunch with Logan, and Paige ate from noon to one, using the break to study while she crammed in a bite.

After returning from the kitchenette, Paige met Ava in the hall, taking Mrs. Mulligan—the one o'clock appointment—into an exam room. The older woman wore a curiously broad smile as she passed by.

When she rounded the corner and found a lavish bouquet of blue hydrangeas on her desk, Paige stopped cold. Then she stepped closer to look for a sign of where they'd come from.

No note or card. Logan must have brought them by for Ava. He was sweet like that. And knowing how rough Paige's day started, Ava probably set them on her desk to lift her spirits.

Since Logan and Ava had started dating, Paige had watched with a little envy how he treated her—always leaving notes on her desk or dropping by just for a five-second kiss, only to be out the door again. No wonder they were already making wedding plans after such a short engagement.

She sat down at her desk. At least she could enjoy the sweet, lingering fragrance of the bouquet for a while.

Twenty minutes later, she heard Ava emerge from the exam room talking with her patient. "I think you must be the picture of health, Mrs. Mulligan. We'll have to get you to do a twelve-hour fast before we perform that triglycerides test, though." Ava draped the stethoscope around her neck. "If you'd like to schedule that, Paige can put you on the calendar. It should be a quick visit since we did everything else today. Just come some morning so you don't have to go hungry throughout the day."

"Why, that's perfect. It'll give me another chance to get to know you and your lovely office staff."

Paige looked up from her computer screen and smiled. "I'm afraid there aren't many of us staff, Mrs. Mulligan. Just me."

"And you must be something special with somebody giving you such a beautiful bouquet of hydrangeas." The woman drew out the word *beautiful* like it was a string of taffy.

"Oh, those aren't mine." Paige directed a nod toward Ava. "Dr. Fenn's fiancé dropped those off."

Ava shook her head. "No, I just had lunch with Logan. He brought me a strawberry banana smoothie, but no hydrangeas."

Mrs. Mulligan's smile stretched until the creases in her cheeks deepened. "You must have an admirer, then." She wagered. "You know what it means to get hydrangeas from an admirer, don't you?"

Paige's eyes widened. "I'm afraid I don't."

"You're just in luck then, because I do. The story goes that centuries ago, a Japanese emperor offered hydrangeas to a beautiful woman as a symbol of his love and as an apology for being so distracted by his work protecting his country. So, hydrangeas are a request for forgiveness. They show regret." She sighed. "Such lovely flowers, don't you think?"

The woman had a flair for storytelling, that was certain.

"How did you come to know that?" Ava asked.

"Oh, honey." Mrs. Mulligan waved at the air. "My husband and I own the Victorian house on the other side of town. When we bought it, I wanted to have an authentic Victorian flower garden in the back—just a little enjoyment for Hugh and me. As it turns out, when I was researching flowers, I discovered the Victorians thought their gardens were too good for hydrangeas. And, to add insult to injury, people thought a woman who grew hydrangeas would never get a husband. Imagine that."

"Wait." Paige cocked her head. "The Victorian house? Isn't that the bed-and-breakfast?"

"Why, yes, it is. You should come sit in the conservatory sometime and visit the garden. We'd love to have you. We've got a fine young man staying with us right now. When I left earlier, he was outside helping my husband with the garden. So kind. I should get back to them now." She slipped her sweater on. "By the way, that picture on your desk." She pointed to the frame. "Is that your daughter?"

Paige smiled and glanced at the photo. "Yes, that's my Emmie."

The woman put a hand to her chest. "She's a living doll. And that dimple in her chin? It's the mark of beauty."

"Thank you." Paige bit her lip. It was the telltale feature she'd gotten from Maddox.

"Well, ladies, I should be getting back. I'll check my calendar at home and call in some time for that triglycerides test." She tilted her head and looked at Paige. "You know, dear, those flowers really do say something."

Paige nodded politely as the woman turned to leave. "Wait, Mrs. Mulligan?"

The woman turned around.

"Your Victorian garden. Did you plant hydrangeas?"

"Of course I did, honey, authenticity aside." She beamed. "I'm of the opinion that forgiveness is an under-appreciated expression we all too often need to exchange. That and, well, I already had a husband." She winked and walked out the door.

Late that evening, Paige pulled into the pebble drive, the third of the girls to arrive at Ava's place. When Ava opened the door, Carly and Jessie were kneeling at the coffee table, pulling the contents of a mani-pedi case out for use.

"Am I late?"

"No." Jessie cocked her head. "Lydia owns that title.. She's coming from the fertility clinic, though. So maybe in a few weeks' time she can claim to be late for a different reason, and I can start getting used to being called Auntie." She wagged her eyebrows..

"Well, we can't exactly chastise her for that, now can we?" Carly snapped up a bottle of berry-red nail polish.

As Ava started to close the door, Lydia called from the porch. "Is that my name I hear?"

"Hey, sis. Yep, we were talking all about you. Jessie tossed a pillow aside to make room for Lydia. "How'd the appointment go?"

"Our doctor was encouraging. We should know something soon."

"That's exciting." Ava hung Lydia and Paige's jackets in the coat closet.

"I'm trying not to get my hopes up, but I'd be lying if I said I hadn't already." She bent to kiss her sister on the head and scooted in beside her. "And Wyatt would tear down a wall tonight if I gave him the go-ahead to remodel for a nursery."

After the girls made their scattered nests on the couch, chair, and floor, they settled into comfortable conversation, shifting to the happenings earlier in the day.

Carly sat back, feet propped on the coffee table with toes spread in pedicure sponges. "So Paige, you really think that woman, Mrs. Mulligan, brought those flowers into the office *for* Maddox today?"

Paige shrugged. "They show up on my desk at the same time she comes in for an appointment. She plugs me with the story of hydrangeas symbolizing forgiveness and regret over excessive military commitment. *And* Maddox is staying at her place. It makes sense to me." She called out toward the kitchen, "Ava, did you not see her bring them in?"

"No, I told you. I was in the bathroom. When I came out, she was in the waiting room, and the flowers were already on your desk."

Carly straightened her toe sponges. "What if you've just got an admirer?"

"That only happens in the movies." Jessie filed vigorously at a fingernail.

"Not true. Don't forget sixth-grade science classes," Lydia added. "Don't you remember Vincent Roundtree?"

Jessie grimaced. "I've been trying to forget for years, but you won't let me. Thank you very much."

"When we were kids, Jessie had the cutest little admirer." Lydia smirked.

"*Little* being the operative word. He stood a full twelve inches shorter than I was, and he stole a kiss from me on the bus one afternoon that left me mortified."

"I'm still surprised he reached your lips."

"If I hadn't already been sitting down, he wouldn't have."

"Poor kid." Lydia laughed. "You dashed his dreams when you decked him for that innocent smooch."

"It was gross. He still had cafeteria pizza breath from lunch."

"She disinfected with some high-octane mouthwash when she got home."

"Story of my life. I either attract men who are gross on some level, too short for my tastes, or both. Maybe I'm just not supposed to find a man."

"I highly doubt that." Carly cocked her head. "It'll happen when you least expect it. Believe me."

"Oh, don't rub it in." Jessie tossed a pillow at Carly. "I'm totally jealous of both you and Ava," Jessie whined. "Men land in your laps. For crying out loud, you literally fly to Chicago, walk up to a guy's door, knock, and *ba-bing*, relationship jackpot. Then, you come home, set Ava up on a blind-date photo shoot, and abracadabra, instant love connection. When's it my turn? That's what I want to know."

Lydia put a hand to her brow as if looking into a bright horizon, "I can see it now. You're luck is about to change. No more fending off short men with pizza breath for you. Although—wait. What's that? There may be an admirer in your future who dumpster dives and has a fetish for strange odors."

Jessie whacked her sister in the face with a pillow and a new round of giggling erupted.

Ava piped up. "Speaking of relationship jackpots, Carly, when do we get to meet Jex?"

"I barely get to see him myself since he's been trying to get his business going in Atlanta, but he may come to town for Thanksgiving. If he does, you guys will be the first to meet him, I promise."

Jessie glanced across the room. "You've been quiet, Paige. Tell us about your guy, Maddox, right? You knew him before?"

Paige shifted, sinking herself lower into the overstuffed chair. "He's not my guy, but he *is* Emmie's father."

Carly's voice softened. "What's the bad blood between you two?"

The smile that had spread across Paige's face just seconds ago, as she watched the girls badger each other, had now dissipated. She hesitated at first, not knowing how much she wanted to share. She'd never really had girlfriends, had kept things to herself her whole life. But then, these women were the most genuine humans she'd ever met, and somehow they made her feel safe entrusting them with the details of her life.

"Maddox and I met a few months before graduation." She began. "At first, I just thought he was a sports jock with a death wish for his reputation. I was never exactly one of the popular girls I'd noticed him hanging around."

"So, he's good-looking?" Jessie asked. Lydia nudged her.

Though he'd always made Paige's heart flutter, she wavered, not willing to throw a gold star in his direction. "He can hold his own. Anyway, I wasn't the most social butterfly in the swarm, but he started walking me home from school in the afternoons the fall of our senior year."

She looked across the room at the girls rapt in her story. "At first, we became good friends. He'd confide in me about how living with his dad was like constantly being in boot camp, and I'd share the trials of being the daughter of a couple of addicts. By the spring, we were pretty much inseparable. Then," she sighed, "I made the mistake of letting him kiss me."

"Kisses change everything." Jessie blew at her nails.

"Yes, I guess they do. Anyway, we knew he'd be leaving soon for the Marines, and we put our feelings on hold for a while after that first kiss. It was one of the hardest things I think I've ever done."

After a deep breath, she hugged her arms. "On graduation night, he took me to a boathouse his family owns, and that's when we didn't hold those feelings back anymore."

A moment passed before anyone said anything.

Then Jessie, her voice now bent with compassion, asked, "What happened when he left for boot camp?"

"I don't know. I think he *wanted* to go into the service, but his dad was more invested in his career path than he was, always pushing him." She shifted. "Anyway, before he left, he told me he wouldn't have a personal phone, nor would he be able to call until his twelve weeks of boot camp were over. I expected that because it was the same with my uncle Robert. He was a Marine too. Anyway, I promised Maddox I would write to him every day, but just before he left, he told me that if I did write often, he would be the standout at mail call. And getting letters every day or two would put him on the drill sergeant's target list even more, especially since he was the son of a colonel."

"The military is so edgy." Carly frowned.

"He gave me his parents' address and arranged for me to send my letters there. He said his dad would forward them through one of his old colleagues."

"Did Maddox write to you too?"

"He claims he did, but I never heard from him again until last Friday."

"What about the phone call after boot camp?"

"It never came. By then, I knew I was pregnant and couldn't keep it from my parents much longer. I was lucky that my uncle Robert was on leave at the time and had come to stay with us for a few days."

Paige stood and walked to the window. She propped her arm on the sill. "When I told my parents, they were furious, made me pack my bags that night. My dad said he'd have no part in paying for another kid. I guess they had enough debts of their own racked up by that point that helping me was too much to ask." She looked back over her shoulder at the girls. "I mentioned they were addicts. My dad was a gambler. Probably still is. And my mom? Well, you could say she was a professional shopper, addicted to spending money."

A sigh escaped her lips. "Uncle Robert saved me, though. He put us up in a hotel for the night, took me to buy some maternity clothes the next day, and rented a tiny little apartment for me to use while he was deployed to Afghanistan. He even gave me the keys to his car." She paused. "In a matter of a few days, he'd helped me get a job at a little donut shop across the street, put enough food in the refrigerator until I could get a paycheck, and left for his tour."

"What happened then?" Ava leaned forward in her chair.

"Three months later, Robert came home in the cargo hold of a plane, and I had to move out." Paige's tone came out dry, emotionless in the same second she teared up. The mood in the room turned even more sober.

"I tried to get in touch with Maddox dozens of times. Tried his parents too. But he never responded. No one ever returned my calls. When I went to where they lived, someone else answered the door. They'd moved. It didn't take long for me to get the picture." She sighed. "I lived in Robert's car for a while. Even drove myself to the hospital the night I went into labor. Then, by the time Emmie came, I didn't want his help anymore."

Paige glanced at the girls and quickly brushed her wet cheek with the back of her hand. "So, Maddox came to Camden Grove because he just found out about Emmie three months ago. His parents had kept my letters from him and convinced him, probably before he even came out of boot camp, that I'd moved on. He saw Emmie for the first time this weekend and found out then that she has Down syndrome."

"Should that matter? Her having Down syndrome?" Ava asked.

"It shouldn't, but I've always wondered if it would."

"How did you do it? Where did you go?" Lydia asked.

"I learned how to become resourceful. We might not have stayed in the prettiest places, but I worked when I could and found the right help for Emmie. There are programs. Then, when I'd saved enough money and filled out enough financial aid forms, I started taking night classes, eventually landed a better job. I met Ava while I was working for Dr. Simmons in Nashville."

Carly shook her head. "Your luck sure didn't change much as an employee of that creep."

"But couldn't you have required Maddox to pay child support?" Jessie asked.

"There were definitely times when we needed the money, but I was so bitter I didn't want to find him, didn't want his money."

Ava stepped to Paige's side and rested a hand on her shoulder. "You've done what's most important. You've given Emmie all the love she could've ever wanted."

"Something still doesn't make sense, though." Carly scooted to the edge of the couch. "You said he found out three months ago. Why didn't he show up then?"

Paige pursed her lips. "I don't know. I don't know what to believe."

"You've got to talk to him." Carly nudged.

"Why? What's left to say?" The edge in Paige's voice sharpened. "He left me."

"When you were younger, did you love him?" Carly continued.

"I did love him . . . fiercely. Before Maddox, I'd never let anybody get that close to me. And I haven't since."

"Maybe he loved you, too. You said he claims he tried to connect with you through his parents after he left?"

"That's what he said."

"That doesn't suggest one-night-stand kind of thinking." Carly shrugged.

"He never *expected* us to be physical. It wasn't like that. He never pushed." Her eyes softened. "When it did happen . . ."

Ava looked at Paige. "Did he say he loved you?"

She drew a long breath. "Yes."

The living room stayed silent for a long few seconds. "Paige, you've worried over this all weekend long. You weren't yourself today in the office, and anybody could tell it weighs heavily on you now. Isn't it worth your peace of mind to at least talk to him and get some answers?" Ava asked.

"That's the million-dollar question, I guess."

The rest of the evening, conversation migrated from topic to topic, as if they all sat at a grand buffet sampling a little here and a little there, until they'd satisfied their appetites.

Paige hadn't been too engaged, though. The question Ava posed continued to needle at her thoughts. She knew her friends were right. If Maddox left Camden Grove, she might never see him again. And there were still things to say, questions she craved to have answered.

On her way to pick up Emmie that night, she drove in the direction of the bed-and-breakfast. She didn't *have* to pass by the old house. She could have taken another route. But by driving past, she wondered if the notion of talking to him would come any easier. It seemed the next closest step, like putting her own toe in to test the water with nobody watching for her reaction.

His Jeep, parked under the pale glow of a post light, left Paige with a twinge of something she hadn't felt in a long time. She slowed the car and eased past the drive, wanting only to summon a little more courage, not to commit altogether.

When she saw his silhouette in one of the upper windows, a surge tingled through her veins. She pushed it away by sheer will, refusing to allow anticipation to evolve into hope. Waiting for answers now somehow felt like an inherent part of her. Tonight, she'd go home, and though she had no illusion that she could prepare herself for no longer waiting, she knew one thing: everything would change starting tomorrow.

Chapter Nine

Maddox

Maddox tossed and turned the whole night, wondering if Glenna's flower delivery had muddied the water even more, questioning if maybe he should have turned down the gesture. Though he'd been concerned when he first recognized her intentions, her enthusiasm about helping wasn't easy to turn away.

By morning, his doubts peaked, and he found himself out in the garden early, ready to work off some nervous energy. The Mulligans hadn't asked for any help. In fact, they protested at first. The upkeep of the old house and garden seemed a hefty undertaking for someone half their age, though, and keeping busy was a good distraction from the worries that continued to nag at him. He didn't want to leave Camden Grove without some sense of settling matters with Paige at the very least, but he was afraid that was exactly where things stood and would remain—unsettled.

After getting directions from Hugh, he spent the morning pruning and digging, weeding and mulching. The Mulligans soon joined him, working in other parts of the garden after the morning warmed under a reluctant sun.

As he snipped at the branches of a small, decorative tree, the work seemed harsh. Cutting off the dead or disorderly in hopes of something new or re-imagined was an act of faith. He wondered if he had enough faith to snip at the deadwood of his own past, doubted he should even loosely look for something new. Still, the approaching deadline for his reenlistment contract kept his expectations aligned with the reality that he already had a well-settled life with comrades and commitments. Why change something that worked?

As the lunch hour approached, the Mulligans went inside to fix sandwiches and rest for a moment. Maddox stayed and continued pruning.

When he first saw Paige enter the garden from the conservatory, his muscles went rigid, and his heart began to race. Through the crimson leaves of a crabapple tree, he watched her gazing awestruck at the elegance of the garden, just as he must've done the first time he'd laid eyes on it.

As she moved closer, a bead of sweat trickled down his back beneath a damp t-shirt. Had he not been warm from working, he'd have surely heated up at the sight of her. The skirt she wore clung to her attractive figure and left him with no inclination to look away.

She meandered the path toward him, taking in the sights, and for an instant, time rolled back. She reminded him of the girl from six years ago, walking home from school, content enough to be alone.

A warm breeze picked up, and a few fortuitous helicopter seeds from the sycamore beyond the hedgerow floated to the ground between them. He resisted moving into view, instead watching her drink in the beauty of the garden path. As she drew closer, her hand brushed the fronds of the tall ferns, like touching them somehow lightened her load. He realized then, looking at her, that he remembered what it felt like to love her. But that was in the past . . . the past. With each step she took, though, he tried less and less to convince himself of that conclusion.

She stopped when she saw him. The space between them felt peculiar, somehow false. "I've never seen a garden like this." Her words broke the ice but came out distant and cool.

She looked past him. He knew, before her expression confirmed it, that she'd spotted, along the back wall of hedges, the bright blue hydrangea bush. She'd likely noticed, too, that someone had snipped a few of its stems.

Maddox nodded. "The Mulligans call it their hidden gem." He propped the clippers in the crook of the tree. "I'm glad you came."

Paige cleared her throat. "I'm not sure why, but I'm here. I'm on my lunch break, so I'll keep it short."

He tried to remain expressionless fearing if he reacted one way or another, it would push her away.

"If you want to talk, I'll meet with you, but it'll be me, alone. I'm not ready for anything more. Do we understand each other?"

"Paige, I'm not here to upset you or Emmie. I just wanted to—"

"I'm not planning on letting you upset either of us. We've started a new life here in Camden Grove, and for the first time, I feel like we've got a chance at being happy. I'm not about to let anybody ruin that for us."

Her words stung, and he offered a more stoic response than he'd have liked. "Understood. When and where do you want to meet?"

Glenna came walking up the path carrying a tray of sandwiches and drinks. "Why don't you two visit here?" She smiled. "I'm sorry," she said as she came closer. "I wasn't trying to eavesdrop. Maddox, here, has been hard at work all morning, and I was just bringing out some sandwiches and lemonade." She raised her eyebrows to Paige. "Are you hungry, dear?"

"No, but thank you. I'm on my way out." She tilted her head toward the bush. "I now see where those beautiful hydrangeas came from. Thank you for bringing them in yesterday. You should've mentioned they were from you. I would've given a proper thank you then."

"Oh, those flowers weren't from me." Glenna smiled and nodded toward Maddox. "Aren't hydrangeas the most healing plant you've ever seen? I just love 'em." She pursed her lips. "Anyway, Hugh and I will be leaving for the evening. There's a new historical film on in Hartley he's taking me to see tonight. You two could have dinner here? You'd have the whole place to yourselves."

Paige folded her arms and appeared agitated. "That'll be fine. Dinner won't be necessary, though." She shifted on her feet and avoided eye contact with Maddox. "I'll leave the office at five and be back in town by six."

When she turned to go, she didn't say goodbye but offered a second concise thank you to Glenna and marched back to the conservatory, her steps charged with the objective of leaving with no delay.

Glenna set the tray on a vine-covered stump and handed Maddox his sandwich wrapped in a napkin. "Looks like you've got yourself a date."

"I don't think Paige would call it that."

"Well, neither you nor Miz Paige yet knows what kind of magic happens inside my conservatory."

Maddox brushed his hands off and took a drink. "I'm just hoping for a little civility. That would be magic enough for me."

"I'll go tell Hugh that we have a dinner menu to prepare." She winked, then turned toward the house.

Maddox started to object, then knew better. He'd already deduced that Glenna didn't take no for an answer when she set her mind to a task.

After finishing the sandwich, he picked up the pruning shears and began again to snip at the deadwood, wondering to himself what the evening would hold.

Chapter Ten

Paige

That afternoon, Ava opened her next patient's file and leaned over the counter to grab a pen from the desk organizer. "Well, how'd it go?"

Paige sat in her office chair, listlessly rolling her mouse in figure eights over the soft pad, working out remnants of anxiety from her lunch hour. "I saw him. We're meeting tonight at six." She looked at Ava. "Well, *if* I can find a sitter for Emmie. I've got to work some things out in my mind before I let him see her."

"She can stay with me. Logan and Toby are coming over tonight to play some board games. We'd love to have Emmie hang out with us."

"That would actually be perfect." Paige bit her lower lip.

Ava propped her elbows on the counter. "You're worried about tonight, aren't you?"

"Way more than I'd like to be."

"Just go talk to him. See what you find out and how you feel after that. Give it some time. You'll know what to do."

"I hope you're right."

"How'd you feel when you saw him earlier?"

Paige touched the base of her neck. "Like . . . I was waiting again, but not for him to call or write. Just waiting for something. It's like I'm in a boat that's always had a leak. I'm tired of bailing and just waiting to sink."

Ava picked up the file folder and stepped to the waiting room door to get her next patient. Her voice softened. "Maybe, with a little time, you'll find that Maddox has the tools to patch that leak." She smiled and called in the next patient.

When Paige arrived at the Mulligans' home later that evening, the gas-style lamp posts that surrounded the house lit up the sidewalk to the front porch, giving the place a warm glow. Several boxes marked *Christmas Lights* sat to the side of the door, waiting for attention. After a few seconds' pause, Paige took a deep breath, shored up her nerves, and knocked on the door.

She heard the shuffling of feet inside and could see through the frosted glass a kaleidoscope of color moving closer. As the door squeaked open, an older man, bent a little with age, greeted her. She hadn't met him when she came to the house earlier in the day.

His sparkling eyes, nearly closed with the weight of his bushy brows, narrowed to thick lines as he smiled and welcomed her inside. "You must be the lit'l miss that Maddox has come to the Grove to see."

Paige stepped into the foyer reluctantly.

"I'm Hugh Mulligan. The wife told me all about yer visit earlier today. Sorry to have missed meeting ye then."

"Paige Westerfield." She held out a tenuous hand. "Nice to meet you."

"Come into the conservatory, Miss Westerfield."

"Please, just Paige."

"Likewise, then, just Hugh." He shuffled in front of her through the hallway and into the massive domed room. She didn't imagine it could have been more beautiful than it was earlier in the day, but the glass conservatory, now lit with white twinkle lights tucked along the vaulted beams, glowed. Beyond the glass and into the backyard, copper foot lamps lit the winding path until they disappeared behind the towering oak.

Hugh interrupted her gawking. "Glenna planned a meal that we made for ye. Hope it's a suited to your tastes."

At the center of the conservatory sat the small round table she'd seen earlier, now draped in a white linen cloth and set with china. To the side, a serving table with a spread of hot food waited.

"This is really too much. I—"

"Nonsense. Ye have to eat, don't ye?" the old man said, effectively quieting her objection.

Paige shook her head. "It's just that we were going to talk for only a few minutes. I hadn't planned for you to make a meal."

"Have ye eaten already?"

Paige paused, reluctance in her voice. "No, after work, I had an errand to run and came straight here."

"Then ye must be hungry."

She scanned the table set with a variety of colorful dishes and couldn't deny it all smelled heavenly.

"Come sit." Hugh shuffled to the table and pulled out a seat. He took her jacket and waited as Paige slid into the chair.

She glanced up at the glass dome once more, glowing in the soft light. "You have a beautiful home. I've passed by several times since I moved here, but I didn't realize you had all this in the back."

"Most don't. Our lit'l refuge, don't ye think?"

"I'll say," Paige spoke to herself more than to him.

Glenna rounded the door from the kitchen with a steaming bowl of vegetables. "Well, hello, honey. You look ready to eat. I'm so glad. We've fixed a few things. Hope you like it."

Paige stood and shook her head. "Mrs. Mulligan, you really shouldn't have. I was just planning on a short visit, that's all."

Glenna chuckled. "And you got more than you bargained for. In my book, that's almost always a good thing." She set the bowl on the table.

"It looks delicious. Thank you."

"Hugh, darlin', will you go tell Maddox his guest is here?"

The old man padded out of the conservatory obediently.

"He should be ready by now. We had to nearly drag him away from the garden and tell him to clean up. He's been out there working all day long. I don't know what we'd have done without him. We wouldn't have gotten the winterizing done, that's for certain." Glenna propped a hand on her hip.

"Yes, well . . ." Paige changed the subject. "How long have you lived here?"

"We bought this house after Hugh retired, twenty-some years ago now. He was a builder, one of the finest craftsmen on God's green earth. He built this conservatory for me for our twenty-fifth wedding anniversary." She raised her hands as if to display the room. "It was an add-on after we bought the place. When I step into this room, something about it brings the quiet back into my soul." Glenna looked at Paige. "You seem to me the kind of girl who likes the quiet things in life. Am I right?"

Paige tilted her head, a little reserved about being so readable.

"No need to be shy about it. It's a wonderful thing. I think that's what gives us the ability to put away the clutter and see clearly."

The sound of steps at the conservatory entry drew their attention as Maddox entered the room, rubbing his stubbled jaw.

"Paige." He acknowledged her in one slow nod.

In her stomach, a flutter of butterflies took flight. She pressed her hands against it, attempting discreetly to calm her nerves. As he crossed the floor, she tried not to stare, but that proved a challenge for which she hadn't really prepared. His dark hair, still damp and spiked, attested to how recently he'd been in water. He wore loose jeans and a casual navy-blue Henley, the muscles of his chest and arms made more obvious by its slim fit. She finally forced her eyes away.

For each of the times they'd seen each other in the last four days, she'd either been shocked or braced against emotional impact. Tonight, though, she found herself under a different spell—one that came unexpectedly. The tension pulsing through her thoughts was measured in equal parts anticipation and reluctance—that same feeling she'd once gotten before boarding a beast of a roller coaster with her uncle Robert.

She cleared her throat. "Maddox."

"Well, now, I hope you two have a wonderful dinner." Glenna smiled. "Hugh and I'll be stepping out now to leave you to your visit. Our movie plays in just an hour. G'night, darlin's."

As she stepped out of the conservatory, the room fell silent.

Maddox held Paige's chair, as Hugh had done, and waited. When she seated herself, he took the chair opposite. "I don't want you to think I asked for all this." He nodded toward the entry. "Hugh and Glenna, well, they're really nice people, and I didn't want to hurt their feelings. I mean, not that it's something I wouldn't want to do with you . . . I just didn't want to make you uncomfortable." He rubbed his jaw again.

"You're nervous." It came out sounding curt.

"That obvious?"

"You used to rub your jaw when you were nervous or didn't want to tell me something." She slipped a linen napkin from the table and smoothed it across her lap. "I learned that the day you told me you were leaving for the Marines."

He nodded once, then looked at the table of steaming dishes. "Maybe we should eat before this all gets cold." Pulling his napkin from the plate, he asked, "Can I serve you something?"

Words burst from her mouth as if she'd been holding her breath. "I just want to set something straight first. If you have any intentions of walking into our lives to change things, assert your parental rights, I'll fight you tooth and nail. I've spent years in survival mode, on my own, so don't assume I'm a pushover."

Maddox leaned toward her, his voice deep and low when he said, "There is nothing in me that has ever wanted to change or take anything from you . . . ever."

After those words crossed his lips, a stillness settled over Paige—not complete peace, but a time-out from the constant apprehension that had followed her since Maddox's arrival. The uncertainty had nearly been unbearable.

Chapter Eleven

Maddox

Maddox proposed they take a moment and enjoy the meal Glenna had prepared without the pressure of talking about the obvious. It would surely come soon enough, and maybe, if they eased into the conversation, they could manage discussing all that had happened a little less awkwardly with a good meal in their stomachs.

At first, they talked stiffly and mostly of innocuous things as they sampled the dishes. They spoke of Camp Lejeune, where Maddox was now stationed in North Carolina, and about how Paige liked living in Camden Grove.

Maddox shared with her some of the responsibilities he held as a Raider. He talked of his team, how all the guys had pulled each other out of more scrapes than he could count. He asked Paige about her job with Dr. Fenn and if she missed Nashville. He'd noticed on Saturday that she was studying at the library, so, he asked about her schooling. She told him of her ambitions to become a nurse practitioner, eventually.

When they'd exhausted all the small talk and tried most everything but dessert, a few awkward moments of silence followed, and their restlessness became too much. Maddox asked if she wanted to step out into the garden. He hoped at least for a steadier rhythm of strained conversation.

The copper foot lamps along the path lit their way for a slow and lingering walk. Finally, Paige drew in a deep breath and asked the first hard question.

"Why didn't you make your own decision about joining the Marines? Did you really even want to join?"

He knew they were coming, all the why questions. Like an applicant internalizing all the best answers before the big interview, he'd mapped out and rehearsed a handful of responses, but in hindsight, every thought seemed grossly inadequate.

"Anything I tell you will sound weak." He scanned the garden, his eyes resting on the shadows. "Paige, all those years ago, I never wanted to leave you, but I did want to join up." He waited, not knowing if she'd detonate with anger or close up like a sun-scalded flower.

A cool evening breeze caused a willow sapling to sweep the grass close to the corner of the hedge. Maddox focused on it to hush his churning thoughts as they continued along the path.

"When we lived back in Treemont, I had one goal in my life—to be a Marine. I wanted to be a Raider. The only problem was my goal wasn't quite the same as my dad's."

"I remember how your father was." Paige's voice sharpened. "I just thought you were bending to him."

"If I'd done that, I wouldn't be a Raider."

"Congratulations." Her voice was curt.

Maddox continued without regard to Paige's tone. "Serving in an elite teams unit wouldn't have been his first choice for me. He wanted a high-ranking officer in his wake. Enlistment, then the Commissioning Education Program, then Quantico. That's where I would have been in OCS, Officer Candidate School. In hindsight, I'm guessing he saw me falling for you and figured he'd get me enlisted, then work on the rest of the plan a step at a time." Maddox stared at his shoes. They looked strange in the light of the foot lamps. He hadn't grown accustomed to the exchange of combat boots for casuals. "Before he passed away, we'd been at odds. When I started charting my own path, he couldn't come to terms with it. He spit at me every Marine motto known to man, telling me I was destined for top brass." He paused. "I wasn't cut from the same cloth, though."

Paige folded her arms. "I'm sorry. About his passing."

Maddox glanced at her and shrugged. "Yeah, well, I guess as high-strung as he was, the heart attack was inevitable at some point."

They continued to walk.

He looked again at the willow sapling. "November 10, 1715. Do you know what day that was?"

Paige didn't answer.

"It's the day my fifth great-grandfather helped form the first two battalions of troops known as the Marines." He huffed. "I knew that date before I knew my own birthday. Grandfathers, uncles, cousins, my dad—they were all Marine officers, retired or killed in action." He kicked at a pebble on the path. "I was the next in line, according to the Colonel, destined for a chest full of medals. It's the whole reason I wasn't supposed to fall in love with you. It might've caused a breach in focus, changed the entire course of Granger history." He turned to look at Paige. "Still sorry?"

She rubbed her arms as if to fend off a chill. "I've had my hard days, but I wouldn't wish bad on anybody because of them. I deserve a little more credit than that. And his disapproval of me was nothing I couldn't have guessed. I knew that the first time I met your parents."

"If it matters, it wasn't you personally that he disapproved of. It was anything or anybody that stood a chance of taking my eyes off the goal."

"But I don't understand why you didn't call. You said that they'd claimed I'd moved on. Did they just pull that conclusion out of thin air? Why just take their word for it?"

His voice sharpened. "Because of what I was told, that's why. Because of what the Colonel showed me."

"What're you talking about?"

He turned away, drew in a deep breath, and continued. "I got your first couple of letters, but after that, the Colonel's colleague stopped bringing them. I thought it was some kind of test my father had conjured up to toughen the kid a little more. I knew you said you'd write and even thought you might come to the graduation ceremony with my parents, but when I asked . . ."

"What?"

"The Colonel showed me a picture he'd snapped of you and somebody else."

"Wait. He was following me?"

"No. He was determined, but not like that. He told me that shortly before they came to Parris Island for my graduation, he'd taken my mother to the mall in Treemont to buy her a new dress for the ceremony. They saw you walking out of a store, arm-in-arm with a man. He snapped a picture with his phone because he knew I wouldn't believe him otherwise."

Her eyes narrowed, searching for understanding. "What? There wasn't anybody else, never has been." Then her jaw went slack as her mind cleared. She whispered, "Robert. It was Robert." Slowly, she shook her head. "You didn't call me because I was shopping with . . . my uncle? He'd just bought maternity clothes for me because I couldn't afford them myself. I even wrote to tell you about all the ways he helped me when I found out I was pregnant. I wrote to you about how my parents kicked me out, and he gave me a place to stay." Tears welled in her eyes. "About how devastated I was when he died in Afghanistan. I wrote to you about all of that."

Maddox lowered his gaze. "I'm sorry." The words felt paper thin.

Paige paced against the mossy stones, rubbing fiercely at her temples. "How could you believe all this? You knew me."

"We were kids, Paige. I knew I hurt you because I left. After seeing that photo, I thought you'd moved on, so I tried to forget."

Paige walked down the path as if she needed space from all she'd just learned. Her back to Maddox, she stopped and stood with her shoulders shuddering in front of the drooping hydrangea bush, now gray in the waning light.

As he approached, she erupted, her hands clenched into fists, veins straining against her skin. She screamed against the limits of a trembling voice, "I've carried hurt and fear of every kind for

Emmie's whole life, and I've done it alone. She hasn't known what it's like to have a mother without regret or resentment or loneliness."

Maddox touched her arm. "I'm sorry, Pai—"

"You could have been there!" She struck at his chest. "You were her father! I had nobody!" Thrashing wildly against his enclosing arms, she finally gave in, slowly melted against him, quaking, until he held her still.

They stood silent for a long time. The night noises and passing cars in the distance beyond the hedge continued as if her outburst had been of no real consequence.

After a while, she pulled away and wiped her face with the back of her hand. "So, you've spent the last three months searching for us, then?"

Maddox had just watched Paige's heartbreak, seen her at her most vulnerable. He swallowed hard, knowing he couldn't allow it to happen again. Not tonight, at least. Healing was a slow process. He would tell her the rest of the story another time. "It took some time to find you."

She stared at the moss at her feet as the seconds passed. Finally, she rounded her shoulders and looked at him. "I guess you want to see Emmie, then."

He measured her expression with his eyes, not truly having expected her to concede. With a deep breath, he gave her an irreversible answer. "Yes. . . .Yes, I do."

She nodded, then put her hand to her head and inhaled her own stuttered breath. "I want to do this slowly and on my terms. No surprises."

"Of course."

"We go to the Memorial Park sometimes on Saturdays, after the library. We'll be there this weekend." She smoothed her clothes. "Meet us at the merry-go-round at two-thirty."

He searched her face for signs—any signs—anger, forgiveness, hatred. Her expression offered nothing but the remnants of the shaken state she'd just been in.

"I'll be there."

Paige looked back toward the conservatory and folded her arms. "I should go. Emmie has school tomorrow."

"I'll walk out with you."

"No. I can find my way. Tell the Mulligans I said thank you for dinner." She replaced her tenuous expression with something new—stoic—and turned her steps to the conservatory, leaving him behind.

As she retreated, the copper sundial Glenna had shown Maddox only the day before, called his attention, glinting under the light of a rising moon.

An hour and a half after Paige left and Maddox had cleaned up the dishes, he heard Hugh's heavy footsteps on the stairs coming toward the Blue Room. The knock at his bedroom door was no surprise. He was sure at least one of the Mulligans would ask about his dinner with Paige.

The hinges creaked as he invited Hugh into the room, his arms loaded with white towels and washcloths.

"Here y'are, my boy. Glenna sent these up, and they smell like a spring rain." He lifted the towels to his nose. "She also told me to tell ye there was no need to do the dishes, though we thought it a kind gesture."

"Thank you for the towels and the meal. Tell Glenna it was delicious." Maddox took the load and set it on the bench at the end of the bed.

Before Hugh had stepped in, the Blue Room felt lonely, but the old man brought in a spark of light.

"I'm guessing your visit was pleasant enough?"

"We talked. That was a step in the right direction, I suppose."

"Well, these things take time. The lasses sometimes set their own path, and we do well just to follow it." He turned toward the door. "I'll let you get some rest."

Before he stepped into the hall, Maddox found himself wanting to delay Hugh's leaving. "Say, you were going to tell me your story of serving in the Congo."

"Aaah, I've told that yarn many a time, but as I get older, I realize that stories of the past some days are to be told and some days seem best left alone. In truth, young man, it's those we tell in our heads—those of a future we can influence—that are really worth our time, don't ye know."

As his words settled like a billowing blanket in Maddox's mind, a sentence he didn't know he was prepared to share flowed from his thoughts through his lips. "Hugh, I have a daughter."

The old man's expression never changed. No judgment or conviction. Only understanding colored his eyes.

"The woman who came here tonight? She's my little girl's mother. I left her six years ago." He clenched his teeth. The muscle in his jaw twitched. "But the worst part is, I didn't know until a few months back I was even a father because I let someone else influence my decisions in the first place."

Hugh stood quietly.

"And when I found out, I waited. For almost three months now, I've waited. No one else to blame for that gap but myself." He walked to the window and peeled back the blue sheers. "I've nearly gotten myself blown up by a roadside blast in Kabul, extracted American casualties from hot spots in Kurdistan, been in every kind of combat situation you could think of, but I've *never* been more scared in my life than I was to come here and face the fact that I'm a father."

He turned to face Hugh. "It took those three months to convince myself to come. Then when I got here, I found out she's a child with special needs. And as bad as it sounds, I'm scared of that too. She's this beautiful little girl . . . got a smile that makes your heart hurt, but I'm supposed to meet her for the first time on Saturday, and I don't even know what to say."

Hugh bowed his head and looked at the floor. "Ma'boy, Glenna and I, we had no children. Not for lack of wantin' 'em, to be sure. But it wasn't in our cards. That part of our story had to be played out differently." He raised his eyes to Maddox. "Now, the way I see it, you're at an advantage. Your story isn't over. Could be that it's just startin'." He smiled. "Six years sounds like a long delay to ye, but truth be told, it's a drop in the ocean. Three months, not even a dabble. And if you're worried about her special circumstance, you're the one moping around about not knowing how to speak to her. My bet is she'll take right off, and you'll do the same." He reached for the doorknob. "Tell ye what, while you're figurin' on it, doubt yer doubts. You'll get it all straightened out. I'm certain of it."

When Hugh closed the door on the way out, Maddox felt as if he'd been left with a book of empty pages and told that his job was not to read the story but to write it. He wondered if he had the mettle to do it.

He lay on his pillow that night staring at the blue ceiling turned gray from the moonlight cutting through the sheers.

Conflicted. He was completely conflicted. Coming to Camden Grove had ultimately been the only answer, even when he wasn't sure of the question. Though meeting Emmie had eventually become his plan, Paige was right—he had no idea what effect it would have on her or anyone else for that matter. But now it was happening—everything was in motion.

Between his fingers, over and over, he rolled the flat buckeye.

Doubt yer doubts.

Hugh's words trickled in and out of his thoughts until deep into the night, until sleep finally claimed him.

Chapter Twelve

Paige

After Saturday Story Hour, Paige kneeled between the stacks, buttoned Emmie's jacket, and pulled the ball cap over her braided hair. "You remember what I told you?"

"That we're meeting. At the playground." Though Emmie's choppy words were never hard to understand, they always had a cadence to them.

"Yes. Do you remember who's coming?"

"Of course." Emmie smiled. "My daddy."

Paige stiffened a little at the intimate title. "And do you remember what I said about—?"

"I don't have. To hug him. Or tell him. I love him." She patted Paige's face. "Don't worry, Mommy."

When she finished buttoning and tucking and stalling with particulars that didn't matter, Paige held Emmie at arm's length and smiled. "You're such a big girl."

Emmie's tongue lay on her bottom lip, the low muscle tone causing it to appear thick.

When she afforded herself those moments to think about the what-ifs, Paige mourned the fact that many people would never choose to see beyond the telltale physical signs of a child with Down syndrome to all the capabilities Emmie possessed.

She'd never known anyone with as keen an intuition. Emmie could always sense the feelings of those around her, more than anyone she'd ever met, something most without genetic anomalies would never develop. And though her baby girl had abilities others didn't, her own heart stretched to aching when she stopped to think that Emmie may never experience some of the best things life had to offer.

After a deep breath, Paige pulled her into a hug until she grunted. Then she stood, put on her own jacket, and shored herself up for the next hour.

The merry-go-round horses, decorated in tassels of purple and gold, floated up and down as they circled in their predetermined path to music and the squeals of children. Paige wondered why Emmie loved the merry-go-round so much. When she'd been a child herself, the horses scared her. Nothing intimidated Emmie, though. Not even a first date with her dad.

Promptly at two-thirty, as they rode for the third time, Paige spotted Maddox crossing the lot toward them. She tried not to look, but her eyes lingered at every turn of the carousel for another glimpse.

This time, he wore a pair of khaki cargo pants, a button-up shirt, and a brown leather jacket that again did little to hide his muscular build. The tingle in her stomach came back.

After the ride came to a stop, Paige helped Emmie off her horse and took her by the hand. She was relieved that they'd stopped on the side opposite of Maddox. As they stepped off the platform, she kneeled beside Emmie. "Ok, sweetheart. It's time. He's here now, just on the other side."

Emmie's eyes lit up. "Let's go."

Paige shored up her nerves and stood.

As they rounded the ride, Emmie pulled away and padded ahead.

"Honey, wait." Paige's voice faded against the restarting music of the merry-go-round, and she walked faster.

As Emmie approached him, he scanned the playground. She threw her arms around his waist in a judgeless hug before he could fully turn to face her.

Stopping mid-stride, Paige tried to reclaim the air that escaped from her lungs. She called out, "Emmie, you should've waited. What if you hadn't found the right person?"

Emmie looked at her from under the bill of her hat. "But this is. My daddy. He cleaned. Our car windows."

For a moment, Paige's breath caught in her throat, and Maddox's lips parted at Emmie's remark.

How had she known?

Before either had time to react, she hugged him again, burying her face in his side. "I love you, Daddy."

The muffled greeting was unmistakable, maybe because the music had faded, or maybe because Paige knew before she even mentioned Maddox's name that Emmie would offer him immediate, unconditional love.

Paige tried to brace herself for his reaction. For his first words. All the way to the park, she'd told herself that if he hesitated, floundered, or flat-out changed his mind and rejected Emmie, maybe it would just make things easier in the long run. He could go back to his life, and they'd go back to theirs. She'd have pieces to pick up, but that wasn't anything she hadn't done before. Only now, here they stood, the three of them by a merry-go-round with nothing left but to face reality in full color.

The moment he kneeled in front of Emmie, everything stopped. Children's squeals, the calliope music of the carousel, time itself. Only after he spoke did sound and thought slog into motion again.

"Well, hello there, Miss Emmie." He smiled as he looked into her face. Without pause, he took her hands in his. "Your fingers are cold." He glanced at Paige. "You know what they say about that, don't you?"

"No." Emmie's eyes opened wide.

"Well, I've heard that a person with cold hands has a very warm heart. I think that definitely must be true with you." He stood and gave a quick nod as Paige took her place beside Emmie. "Thank you for letting me come."

Paige stuttered, "W-well, Emmie wanted to. I let her make the final decision."

He kneeled again. "Then, thank you, Emmie, for deciding to see me."

"Of course. I want to see you. You're my dad." She shrugged her shoulders as if the alternative were the most ridiculous notion on the planet. "You wanna play?" Emmie asked.

"I think I'd like that a lot." Maddox unbuttoned his jacket. "Let me set this over on the bench."

Paige held out her hand. "I'll take it."

They exchanged lingering glances, and his lips mouthed another thank you as he handed her the jacket. Emmie took him by the hand.

For the better part of an hour, Paige sat on the bench and watched as Emmie squealed in delight alongside the other children, descending the slide and landing in Maddox's arms again and again. The sound was surreal. She'd heard playground noises many times, but never this. Never *her* child landing in the arms of a dad.

Chapter Thirteen

Maddox

When Emmie had first embraced him at the merry-go-round, Maddox's world spun. The last thing he'd expected was that she knew him from the filling station days earlier. But maybe the biggest surprise was that she'd forgiven him. That she didn't even act as if there were anything to forgive. She only had love to offer. It was the purest selflessness he'd ever felt.

She'd looked into his eyes and proclaimed that she loved him. That he was her daddy. And with those words came a wave, simple but powerful, that swallowed up all the uncertainty he'd possessed in getting ready to meet her.

After a while, Emmie found a friend on the playground. She went up to the little girl and said, "You wanna meet. My daddy?" Maddox could hear their conversation. He sat down at the bottom of the slide to listen.

The friend took little interest, but Emmie persisted. "He's there—" she pointed "—his name's Daddy."

Maddox waved at the little girl from the bottom of the slide. The friend waved back, but instead of obliging Emmie, she jumped on a swing. Emmie followed.

As he continued to watch the two girls, he thought about the sound of someone calling him Daddy. He'd had a few titles in his life—all to do with the military—but this one somehow settled into his mind like some lost rite of passage he didn't know he'd missed . . . hadn't earned.

He turned and saw Paige sitting on the bench in the sunlight, more beautiful than the day he'd first met her. He wondered why she hadn't gone on to marry someone else, why she'd waited. She certainly could have had her choice. When he looked back at the little girls playing, he knew why.

She wouldn't take the risk of hurting Emmie.

Since those years in high school, Paige's slender frame had taken on more curves, all in the right places and proportions. Her hair had grown longer, not the sandy brown bob she'd worn back in school, but now past her shoulders and a bit darker. And her skin was still as smooth and flawless as it had always been. Though the years had no doubt been stressful, in every way he could see, they'd been kind.

When he decided to come to Camden Grove, he didn't know why he hadn't fully prepared himself to be attracted to her again. Maybe he couldn't prepare for it. Maybe he was too focused on the fact that he had a daughter. Could've been that he assumed he'd find the high-school version of that girl—the one he'd grown out of—frozen in time, never having changed. If he were honest, though, she'd aged perfectly, and he now struggled with more than getting used to a new title.

After a few more minutes, he walked across the playground and took a spot beside Paige. They waited together silently as the two girls swayed in the swings and talked amid the other kids playing a game of tag.

He finally spoke. "When did you know?"

"What? About her having Down syndrome? Just after she was born." She stared ahead, never taking her eyes off Emmie.

Maddox bowed his head. "Were you alone?"

"Completely."

He drew in a deep breath and let it go. "I'm sorry, Paige. If—"

"You know, Maddox, I've spent years examining the ifs, and it's really a waste of time." Paige's words sliced with the precision of a scalpel.

They sat silent again.

Then she continued. "They whisked her away the minute she came out. She had breathing problems. A lot of tubes and wires. After they got her stabilized, before they let me see her, they told me. I kept thinking they had to be wrong, but her sweet little face . . ." Paige's voice trailed off.

She folded her arms. "When I was pregnant, I used to think I would have the smartest kid. I would teach her the alphabet and how to read when she was tiny and play learning games with her." Paige smiled at nothing, or no one in particular. "There I was, the cliché incarnate: a kid having a kid. But, at least, I could show the world. My baby would prove that something smart and amazing could come out of a stupid choice."

"Paige, I—"

"Don't." She cut him off. Gazing toward Emmie, she continued. "Then, Emerson was born. She had this angelic face and light, wispy hair. When I was allowed to hold her, all tangled in those tubes and wires, they'd put a tiny pink bow in a lock of that wispy hair as if that might soften the hard truth. And honestly, it did. I looked into that baby's eyes and cried until the well dried up. But then, something about her with that little pink bow in her hair gave me courage."

Paige shrugged her shoulders. "As she grew, she taught me that intelligence isn't just the ability to work a complex math problem or understand a physics law. It's knowing how to love and share and empathize." She nodded toward Emmie at the swings. "She's seen me cry and has wrapped her arms around me at just the right time. She's experienced my worry about finances, of being alone, of wondering about the future, when I haven't spoken a word to her about it. And how do I know that? Because every time, she comes to me at exactly the right moment and tells me I'm the perfect mom for her."

Maddox bowed his head. "Look, Paige, I know I'll never be able to make up for not being there."

"No, you won't." Her voice wasn't angry. Only resolved.

"What can I do, then?"

"About what?"

"Being a little part of your lives. Is there any way we can . . . start from here?"

Paige turned to him. "Maddox, I agreed to your meeting Emmie, but maybe I didn't think this through."

"Why do you say that?"

"When you showed up in Camden Grove, you took me by surprise. But, after thinking about it, I knew that seeing you here meant I was closer to closing the book on that part of my life, and oddly enough, I was actually relieved that maybe I could look you in the eye and put the past away forever."

She shook her head. "Then here, today, I thought you'd meet her and be ready to jump ship again. And honestly, how do I know you still won't? All I know is that I've got a little girl who now thinks she has someone she can call Dad, and I'm going to have to scrape up the pieces when you leave."

"It won't be that way."

"Oh, so you can promise Emmie that you'll be here at all her birthdays, that you'll be around to celebrate the holidays with her or to take her for ice cream when she has a crummy day?"

Maddox looked away. "You know I can't promise those things."

"Exactly. So, I think it's best for her if we're realistic and look at this story without the cozy ending. I can give you our address. You can send Christmas and birthday cards. Maybe we can even schedule an occasional phone call. I just think that's best."

"How am I supposed to agree to that?"

Paige spun around on the bench. "It's easy."

His voice was deep, steady, and calm. "You just introduced me to this most amazing little girl. And she's loving and pure. I didn't know what to expect when I came here today. I'll be the first to admit that I was scared, still am. But, when I hoped for forgiveness, instead, she made me feel like there was nothing to forgive. I wished for the awkwardness to be tolerable, but she made me feel accepted. Paige, I can't bury the past. I don't want to. That would invalidate everything you two have been through, but I can't look Emmie in the eyes now and live with myself later if I only send her a couple of cards a year or make an occasional phone call."

"What do you want from me? If you think you're going to waltz into our lives and start dictating—"

"I told you I wouldn't do that, and I'm not trying to." Maddox leaned back on the bench. "I just," he sighed. "I wish things could be different, that's all."

She shook her head, her tone of voice a combination of exhaustion and resignation. "They're not different, Maddox. Things are not different. Believe me, I laid claim to that wish a long time ago, and it amounted to nothing." Finally, she turned to face him. "Look, I don't think we're accomplishing anything here. Maybe it would be best if we just—"

"No, don't go." Maddox took her hand in his, held it there, compelling her to stay. "Please. Let me, maybe . . . take Emmie to get an ice cream cone. I just want to spend a little time with her. With you." He leaned closer, swallowed. "I can follow you there. We can all meet over at the Creamery on the square. My treat."

Paige looked at Emmie, now sitting alone at the swings, her head leaning against the chain. She pulled her hand from his. With her lips pressed into a tight line, she shook her head. "I don't know, Maddox. This may be too much for her."

"Please. If we get there and you feel like she's getting overwhelmed, you can just say the word."

She glanced at Emmie again, and after a few long seconds, turned to him. "Fine. But I have other things to do. It'll have to be short."

"I promise, just a few minutes to eat a cone."

Paige called across the playground to Emmie. She skipped clumsily to her mother's side. "Hey, Mommy. Are you having. Fun with Daddy?" The new name still sounded so foreign.

Paige ignored the question and kneeled in front of Emmie. As she re-buttoned the little girl's jacket, she smiled. "It's time for us to go now, but your . . . Maddox thought it might be nice to stop by the ice cream shop for a few minutes. Would you like that?"

Emmie smiled until her eyes squinted. She wrapped her arms around Paige's neck. "You bet."

"Ok." She stood and turned back to Maddox. "We'll meet you there, then."

"Can we go. In the same car. Mommy?"

"I think it would be best for us to drive separately."

"Can I go. With Daddy, then?"

"You should go with me, honey."

"Pleeease?" Emmie pleaded.

"You could ride right behind us, Paige." Maddox interrupted. "It's not too far."

She looked at Maddox, then at Emmie, and hesitated a second too long.

"I promise. To buckle up." Emmie again hugged her mother around the waist.

Paige took a deep breath and frowned at Maddox. "In the back seat. In the middle. And I'll have to get the booster seat."

Emmie turned to Maddox and raised her hand for a high five. He obliged.

"Can we talk?" Emmie's voice carried over the back seat to Maddox driving toward the Creamery.

"You bet." He smiled at her grown-up question as he watched her through the rearview mirror. "What would you like to talk about?"

"My mommy."

"Okay," he answered, his voice laced with caution. "Shoot."

"Do you. Love her?"

Maddox wasn't prepared for the conversation to be so direct. "I think your mommy is beautiful, just like you are. A few years ago, before you were born, I loved her very much."

"But you left?"

"Yes . . . I had to leave." Maddox looked out the window at the passing trees.

"Do you. Love her now?"

"You ask some hard questions."

"That's what. Mommy says. I asked her, too."

"You asked her if she loved me?"

"Yep."

His curiosity got the best of him when Emmie didn't elaborate. "And what did she say?"

"She did. The same as you."

"What do you mean?" Maddox's eyes shifted from the road to the rearview mirror.

Emmie looked out the window then. "She didn't answer."

Maddox smiled and pulled into the same slanted parking space at the creamery that he did on the day he first arrived in Camden Grove. "Are you ready for some ice cream?"

"Yeah." Emmie began wiggling in her seat.

As Paige pulled in beside them, Maddox unbuckled Emmie and helped her from the car.

"What's your favorite. Flavor, Daddy?" Emmie asked as Paige met them at the shop door.

"Hm, I've always been a caramel praline man myself."

The little girl's face lit up. "That's mine too."

Maddox opened the door as he caught the restless look percolating in Paige's eyes.

Chapter Fourteen

Paige

As they approached the ice cream counter, Paige saw the worker's face brighten at the sight of Maddox.

"Hey, I see you found your friend. You come to collect on what I owe you?"

"Nah, I'm paying. We'll keep the freebie on my tab for a time when I forget my wallet. How's that?"

Feeling out of the loop, Paige scanned the selection of flavors beneath the counter glass.

"What can I get you, then?"

Maddox turned to Emmie. "You like sugar cones or waffle?"

"Both. Sugar this time." The little girl swayed back and forth as she answered.

"Two sugar cones with caramel praline and whatever the lady wants."

Paige shook her head. "No. I'm fine."

"Come on." Maddox urged. "Ice cream? Coffee? Anything."

Paige glanced at the ice cream again. "I'll have a scoop of peach mango sorbet in a cup." She turned to Maddox. "And I'm paying for mine."

Maddox shrugged at the girl behind the counter.

Emmie trotted off to a booth next to the window as Maddox and Paige followed with the ice cream. When they were seated, Paige asked, "So, you've been here before?" She nodded toward the store worker.

"Yeah." He took a bite of ice cream. "I stopped in the other day to get a cup of coffee and ask where I might find you."

Before the conversation got any further, Emmie took an enthusiastic first lick and dumped the scoop into her lap, which then rolled to the booth seat and onto the floor.

Paige and Maddox both scrambled for the napkin dispenser, but it was empty on both sides. Maddox reached over the booth to the next table as Paige stepped back up to the counter.

"Hey, could I get some napkins, please?" She looked at the worker's name tag—*Gabby*.

With a stack in hand, she hurried back to the table. Maddox had sufficiently smeared caramel all over Emmie's jacket by then.

"Here, sweetheart." Paige huffed as she dabbed at the sticky mess. After she finally got Emmie cleaned up and Maddox had mopped the melting scoop up from the floor, Gabby arrived at the table with more ice cream.

"Thought you might need a fresh scoop."

Maddox smiled. "Thanks, Gabby." He got his wallet out, but the girl waved it off. "No charge." She handed a cup with a large scoop and a cone propped on top to Emmie. "It's a topsy-turvy."

"What's a topsy. Turvy?" Emmie asked.

"You get a little bigger scoop in a cup with a cone on top." Gabby leaned in as if sharing a confidence. "I dump mine out all the time, but this little trick helps."

Emmie offered the girl a wide smile. "Thank you."

"You're welcome." She nodded once. "You got a pretty cool ice cream partner, you know."

Beneath a cream mustache and a white, cream-tipped nose, Emmie grinned. "Yeah."

Paige interrupted. "Do you think we could get a wet dishcloth to wipe the seat? It's pretty sticky now."

"Sure," Gabby said. "I'll be right back."

She swiveled on her heel toward the counter and, after returning with the cloth, wiped down the seat. Emmie smiled. "Mommy, you should. Sit with Daddy now. Beside me will. Be all wet."

Gabby glanced at Paige as if questions were forming in her thoughts. "I should have grabbed a dry towel. I can get one if—"

"No." Emmie smiled. "Mommy. You can sit. With Daddy. He won't bite."

Maddox and Gabby hid grins while Paige stood for a second, debating the degree to which she wanted to make this more awkward than it already was. Finally, she scooted into the booth beside Maddox without another word.

She thanked Gabby, who left them to their ice cream. Then she watched as Maddox wiped some leftover stickiness from Emmie's jacket. He wasn't frustrated or angry. Instead, he smiled and put an extra napkin on the table beside her.

"Here ya go, Em."

Paige had never cut Emerson's name any shorter than Emmie. She was surprised to hear Maddox call her Em. Something she'd envied in her classmates growing up was that they all had multi-syllabic names that anybody could shorten with a cute little endearment, making them feel like they belonged. Jackson became Jax; Julia, shortened, was Jules; and Ashley, Ash. Like they all belonged to the Cool Kids Club of People with Reduceable Names. The name Paige couldn't be shortened. She didn't really belong anywhere.

For a moment, hearing the short, warm sound of the name Em cross his lips made Paige feel like Emmie was special, like someone finally realized the value of including her. That tugged at her a little, probably more than she wanted to admit.

Instead of thinking too much about it, she reached for her spoon, took a bite of peach mango, and stole a glance at Maddox and Emmie enjoying the same flavor of ice cream.

"How long are you here?" Paige asked, more so that news of his leaving came to Emmie from him instead of her. Though she was curious.

Before he could answer, Emmie's eyes lit up. "Yeah. When can you. Come over?"

"Oh . . . well, I'm not sure." He paused and licked his cone.

Paige took the opening to interject. "Honey, Maddox probably has to get back to his job soon."

"Yeah, I, uh, have to . . . go back to base in a few days."

"A few days? Then you can. Come over. Sooner."

Smiling, he reached across the table and, with a simple act of kindness, picked up the napkin and wiped the ice cream off the tip of Emmie's nose. Paige would have ignored it until they were finished. Somewhere along the line, after so many meals of continuously wiping face and clothes and hands, it just got easier to wait until the eating was over to clean up.

Something about his gesture, though, his attention to that tiny detail, softened her, weakened even more of her hard spots.

"Emmie, can I tell you something?" Maddox asked.

"Sure."

"It's a little secret." He cupped his hand in pretense to hide his words from Paige. "I think your mom might think it's a bad idea. And maybe she's right."

Paige's stomach tied in knots. *Here it comes. He's going to break her heart.*

"Why?" Emmie moved closer.

He dropped his cupped hand to the table. "Well, you may want to ask her about that when you two are alone, but I know she wants you not to be sad. I think she may worry that, since I came to see you and I'll have to leave again, it'll make you sad."

"Of course. I'll be sad. But I still. Want to see you."

The breath Paige held slowly escaped, and the shell around her heart cracked a little.

"Mommy, can't he. Come over?"

Paige hesitated, opened her mouth, and spoke, but she couldn't believe the words that came out.

Later that evening, as Paige emptied Emmie's book bag, she shuffled through a stack of wrinkled coloring pages, a multitude of lines and strokes bleeding outside the borders of each picture she unfolded.

After a while, she sat back in her chair, emotionally drained from the day, a thousand thoughts rolling through her mind. She wondered what effect the visit with Maddox had on Emmie. What effect it had on her. Remembering the look on Emmie's face when he told her she had a warm heart, when he called her Em, or cleaned the ice cream from her nose left Paige with the painful impression that the day had amounted to a little girl falling in love with the idea of having a present daddy.

By letting him in, had she just jeopardized what stability they'd found in Camden Grove? Allowed room for fallout when this man would be a dad in name only? And what was she thinking, agreeing to another meeting? It was too much to process.

Paige sighed and pulled Emmie's day-and-a-half old lunch from the backpack. Tucked at the bottom of the bag, she found the last crumpled item: a flyer announcing some PTA-sponsored fundraiser she had no time or funds for. She tossed it in the drawer where she kept all the school papers, vowing to look at it when she had more energy.

From its landing spot, she took a second glance. The color-printed announcement invited students and their honored guests to Camden Grove Elementary's annual Father-Daughter/Mother-Son Winter Cotillion. A weight pressed down in the hollow of her stomach, and she slammed the door shut just as Emmie came into the room.

"Mommy? Is something wrong?"

"No, honey, of course not." She wrapped her arms around Emmie and pulled her into her lap. "Are you about ready for story time?"

She nodded and, without warning, said, "Daddy thinks. You're beautiful."

"What?" A little shudder of electricity ran through Paige's blood.

"He thinks. You're beautiful."

"Why do you say that?"

"He told me. When I was. In his car."

Thoughts swarmed in Paige's head. "Did he say anything else?"

"Yes. Will you read? To me now?"

Emmie scooted out of her lap and skipped down the hall. Paige followed. "Honey, what else did Maddox say?"

Climbing into her bed, Emmie pushed her library book into Paige's lap as she sat down in a bedside chair. "He told me. That he. Loved you."

As Paige read aloud the words to the storybook, they echoed through the room but formed no plot or purpose in her mind, not like they did for Emmie. The only story that formed fully in her thoughts was one that began a long time ago, under a tree, before she ever dreamed of reading fairy tales to a little girl.

Chapter Fifteen

Maddox

After the ice cream stop and an hour-long chat with Paige and Emmie that evening, Maddox emptied the Jeep of another half tank of gas, riding through the countryside, thinking about them. Thinking about the reenlistment form that waited for him back at the Mulligans'. About his men who depended on him.

Confused thoughts gave way to a certainty that only yielded to turmoil again. He finally pulled into the drive at the Mulligans' resigned for the moment to do only what he'd promised Emmie and Paige, and to wait for clarity to come.

When he stepped inside, he followed the sound of an old Victrola and found Hugh and Glenna dancing in the conservatory. He stood in the shadows at first, watching them sway quietly to a scratchy tune he'd never be able to name. Something in the music, the conservatory, the twinkle lights hanging above them, settled him, gave him a strange sense of hope.

He then slipped away and retreated upstairs, taking care to avoid the creaky spots on the steps he'd come to notice.

The approaching days of winter were beginning to cut short the daylight, so his blue room had taken on the color of slate gray. He could see the glow from the lamps in the garden ruminating over the high hedge-fence beyond his window.

As he hung his jacket on the door peg, the hope he'd just felt dissipated when he saw the file on the corner desk.

He'd come to Camden Grove with a dual purpose: to find Paige and Emmie, and to make a career decision. He fulfilled one of those purposes just hours ago, but in doing so, complicated the other.

Leaving Paige and Emmie that evening was harder than he'd expected. Emmie wanted them to spend the rest of the day together, and the longer they visited, the more Paige seemed to warm up. She even smiled a time or two.

As they were leaving the Creamery, Emmie had begged for him to come home with them. Instead, they left with the agreement that Maddox could meet them at the little chapel on the south side of town the next morning. Paige had admitted to never being a regular church attendee, but she knew it would be good for Emmie to develop some friendships in the area. She said that Sunday church in the South seemed like a prime place for such ambitions.

He suspected that Paige also wanted a neutral place to meet again, that allowing him into their home still seemed too intimate for what she was willing to accept. Either way, he'd take what she had to give in hopes that the clarity he was searching for would come. The file on the corner desk demanded it, and soon.

That night, he accomplished nothing but using Glenna's guest room iron to press a pair of dockers and a fresh button-up for church the next day.

When Maddox came down for breakfast the following morning, the scent of all the regular southern dishes wafted through the house, and Glenna had arranged a new pattern of china on the table in three place settings. She set the last of the serving dishes on the table as Maddox stepped into the room.

"G'mornin' to ye, lad," Hugh piped up with a smile squinting his heavy eyes.

"Good morning."

Glenna placed a butter dish in the center of the table. "I trust you slept well?"

"A little."

"The mattress giving you trouble?" Hugh's eyes twinkled.

"No. Got a few things on my mind. That's all."

Glenna motioned for him to sit. "Oh, and how did your visit go yesterday? What did you think of that sweet little girl?"

Maddox had suspected Hugh would share with his wife what he'd learned of their guest's past. He had no notion it would be a secret. "Emmie is . . . amazing. About the most perfect human being I've ever met."

Glenna sighed and touched her heart. "I already knew you'd fall in love with that child. Her mother, too, of course. They're both just the sweetest."

Confused, he asked, "How have you gotten to know them?"

"We've seen them a few times when we've attended church up at Camden Grove Chapel, and when I visited the clinic the other day, I asked Miss Paige about that darlin' little angel. She has some of your handsome features, you know. That smile and that little dip in her chin? Just adorable."

"Well, I'm sure the best ones come from her mother. That's where I'm headed this morning—to the chapel. Emmie wanted me to come. Are you going?"

"Not today. Hugh's feeling a little worn from working on the Christmas lights. He spent the afternoon yesterday trying to get decorations put up. It's quite the job. I think he tuckered himself out."

"We're on the Christmas tour, ye know. Plenty of lights to string."

"I can help you with that."

Glenna waved off his offer. "Pshhh. You've got more important things to tend to, like winning that girl's heart."

"That may not be in the cards."

Reaching across the table, Glenna squeezed his hand. "Of course it is, dear. You've just got to find your way."

Before he could respond, the Mulligans both bowed their heads, and Glenna began to pray. She included in her petition a request that the Almighty smile on the efforts of those with relationship quandaries.

It couldn't hurt, Maddox thought.

Chapter Sixteen

Paige

At five minutes after noon, the church doors opened, and people spilled out of the chapel like an oozing stream of lava, hot off the bed of a volcanic sermon. The pastor stood on the steps shaking hands, and after Paige, Emmie, and Maddox exchanged the requisite handshake, they migrated toward the parking lot along with the smattering of others making their way home.

As they approached their cars, a voice from the congregation called from behind, "Excuse me, sir."

Maddox, walking hand-in-hand with Emmie, turned around. A plain-looking woman, wearing an outdated jacket and her hair in a bun, approached him. She looked to be in her fifties but aged beyond that by the circles under her eyes. "I'm sorry. I don't mean to bother you. I just wanted to say thank you."

Maddox's brow stitched together in a look of confusion. "Thank you?"

"Yes," the woman pointed over her shoulder to a couple of teenagers standing against a column talking. "That girl over there is mine."

Maddox looked past the woman and saw Gabby, the Creamery store worker.

"She told me what you did to help her a few days back." The woman fidgeted. "Gabby never has been one to make friends easily. Always seems to be the one the other kids find to pick on. But she told me about the other day, and I just wanted you to know that your kindness has changed some things for her." She glanced back and tilted her head. "She's trying a little harder to make friends now, and those other kids . . . well, they've been leaving her alone."

Maddox smiled.

"Anyway, what you did mattered, not only to her but to me."

"Gabby seems like a great kid." He held out his hand.

The woman took it in hers as her eyes fluttered against swelling emotion. Then she gave a quick nod, turned, and left without another word.

As they started back toward their cars, Paige asked, "What happened with that girl from Dawson's?"

"Just some kids showing off for each other, making some jabs at her expense."

"And what did you do?"

He shrugged. "I stopped it."

His smile left her still wondering as they weaved between parked cars. She purposely lagged behind and watched as Maddox walked, hand-in-hand, with Emmie by his side, stiffly skipping two steps to his one. As she considered them, Gabby's mother and what she'd said filtered in and out of her thoughts.

What Maddox did mattered . . . changed things.

She tried to shake the notion from her head that he'd been somebody's champion, only because she had to think of this whole situation objectively, for Emmie's sake. And for her own sake—if she were being honest—she simply couldn't fall for him again.

As they reached the car, Emmie turned and asked, "Mommy. Can we go. On the tracks?"

"Oh, honey, I don't know. Today might not be the best day for the tracks?"

"Why not?"

Paige looked at Maddox and back at Emmie. The truth was, she didn't really have a valid reason to say no. Other than maybe risking her need to stay objective. Her entire philosophy in mothering Emmie had been to say yes when she feasibly could because there would be enough noes in her life. But what about this time?

"What's the tracks?" Maddox asked.

Emmie bobbed up and down with excitement. "Behind the church. Down a road. Are railroad tracks."

"Sometimes, after the Sunday service, Emmie and I take a short walk. There's an old road behind the chapel that leads to an abandoned train track. It's a nice place for a stroll."

"Can we? Pleeeease?"

Paige hesitated, then looked at Maddox again.

"I'm in," he smiled.

After changing their Sunday shoes for the tennis shoes she kept in the trunk, Paige and Emmie led Maddox through the grass to the back of the chapel. The service road, overgrown in the middle with plantain weeds and the occasional brown-capped thistle, still had tire trails clear enough to negotiate the path on foot to the old train tracks.

In the last couple of days, a subtle temperature drop and the gradual surrender of the greenest traces of summer to fall offered the perfect setting for a quiet Sunday afternoon walk. As they came to the end of the lane, the abandoned tracks, which butted against the old road, provided a clearer walking trail.

Levied at a slight incline above the road, access to the tracks required a short climb up a rock bank. Maddox first scaled the bank, and then he reached down for Emmie's hand. She squealed as he pulled her into the air and swung her onto the tracks, landing her gently on one of the broad, weathered railroad ties. Her laughter, carefree and euphoric, opened wide the guarded door to Paige's heart.

Maddox turned back and extended his hand for hers. "You still smile with your eyes," he said.

Taken a bit off-guard, she lingered a moment, then reached for him.

He pulled her onto the tracks beside him with little effort and steadied her with a hand on her waist. His touch sent a sensation through her she hadn't felt since that night at the boathouse over six years ago, a warmth that remained after his hand slipped away from her side.

Emmie awkwardly skipped ahead from tie to tie, stopping occasionally to pick a dandelion or throw a rock. Maddox and

Paige sauntered at a slower clip behind her, listening to the rustle of dried leaves among the tulip poplars lining the tracks.

"You've made an impression on people around here." Paige broke the silence between them.

"What do you mean?"

"The girl from the ice cream shop and her mother, the Mulligans, Emmie. There's no shortage of kudos for you, from what I can see."

Maddox looked down the tracks toward Emmie. "I'm not here trying to make an impression. Just trying to do what's right."

Paige kept her eyes focused ahead. "I don't know yet what I'm ready for, Maddox. This has all happened so fast. I'm trying to let the dust settle before we decide about how to move past today."

"Of course. I'm not rushing. I just want you to know . . . I'm here."

Those two words nearly broke her. How she'd longed to feel that over the years—that he was *here*. But it never came.

Until now.

She stopped and faced him. "For how long, Maddox? Until leave is over and you have to go back to base? Until the next mission takes you somewhere that you may not return from? How long are you here?" Her words weren't sarcastic or confrontational, not even edged in bitterness, just questions that entreated an answer.

"I can't make any promises, Paige. You know that. But please . . . let me at least be here in other ways. I can have things set up so Emmie's provided for in case anything happens and help support her . . . *and* you."

She slowly shook her head, looked away, and began to walk again. He took her by the hand and pulled her back. "You're just as stubborn as you ever were, Paige Westerfield." He shook his head. "But you're so incredibly beautiful."

Before she could pull herself together to respond, Maddox smiled, let go, and turned toward Emmie, jogging to catch up with her. When he reached her, he swung Emmie into the air and set her on his shoulders. It was a sight that caused Paige's heart to ache and soar and break and mend. She continued to walk behind them and listen to Emmie's giggles and wondered how much longer she could hold out before she gave in to any of the old feelings that had started cropping up.

A few minutes later and a half-mile up the tracks, they stopped at a spot overlooking a small pond running parallel to the old railroad. Maddox slid Emmie from his shoulders, and they crouched to pick up rocks to throw into the water.

Emmie liked the big ones, but he coached her to look for the small and flat ones for skipping. Her eyes lit up when he sent his first stone across the water, hitting the surface in a series of quickening taps, then sputtering to a stop and sinking.

As Paige caught up, she stopped within a few feet and watched as he tried a second time to help Emmie find a good skipping rock.

"That's a pretty big one. Here," he said, pulling something from his pocket, "see if you can find one that looks kind of like this. See, it's smooth and almost flat."

"Is that a rock?" Emmie asked.

"No, this is something a little more special."

At first, when Paige saw Maddox turn the flat seed over in his fingers, the memory of it tugged at her only modestly. Then, like the rush of a broken dam, recollections rolled over her. Memories of her very first day with Maddox, of their conversation at the foot of the buckeye tree years ago, of breaking open seedpods and laughing about some Pocahontas jibe. The air around her thickened, and her throat constricted.

"It's a buckeye," she whispered.

He kept it. All these years, he kept it.

"Yes," he smiled and looked at Paige. "A buckeye. It's for good luck."

A while later, back at the parking lot, all the churchgoers had left, and the only vehicles still in the lot were Paige's compact and Maddox's Jeep. As they reached her car, Paige opened the back door for Emmie.

"Daddy, come eat. Dinner with us. Taco lasagna."

Maddox crouched on the ground beside her and began picking off the dry hitchhikers that had clung to her shoelaces and tights. "Don't guess I've ever heard of taco lasagna before."

"It's the best. Mommy made it. This morning. Come, eat with us."

Maddox glanced from Emmie to Paige.

"I just whipped it up because I had the ingredients." She then turned to Emmie, a nervous flutter quivering in her stomach. "He probably has something else to do today, honey."

Maddox rubbed his jaw, the soft sound of fingers scraping over sandpaper. "Mm, actually . . . I don't." He looked at her, hopeful.

"Mommy's taco lasagna. Is. *The best.*" Emmie rubbed her hands together. "You'll love it. Can I ride. With you?" She wrapped her arms around his waist as he stood.

"How about we let Maddox go change out of his church clothes, and maybe he can come later this afternoon? We can save the taco lasagna until then."

"I'd love to." Maddox high-fived Emmie's outstretched hand.

Riding home, Emmie hummed from the back seat her own version of a hymn they'd sung earlier in church. Her soft murmuring, rising and falling in an uneven cadence, faded into the background as Paige thought about the walk on the tracks.

About how Maddox treated Emmie.

About the buckeye.

About his hand on her waist.

She didn't know why she'd postponed his coming home with them until later in the afternoon. Maybe she needed a moment to collect her thoughts, regroup, get some distance, and shore herself up. Why then was she suddenly thinking of what she'd wear?

All this felt so strange. Calm almost. Not in the sense that everything was right. Not like things were normal or orderly, definitely not perfect, but they were something else.

In those seconds he'd taken her by the hand and called her stubborn, and when he'd skipped rocks with Emmie and taken the buckeye out of his pocket, the world had slowed down, everything finding a new rhythm. And for the moment, she didn't know what to make of it. But she felt herself emerging from emotional trenches dug deep and beginning to welcome the new pace.

As she pulled onto their street, Maddox's words came back to her, soaked into her heart like a soft, warm liquid. Words that didn't come secondhand from Emmie this time.

He'd called her beautiful.

The remnants of taco lasagna clung to the sides of a casserole dish as Emmie slid down from the table and ran off to the living room to play with her dolls.

The conversation had been cordial, comfortable even, as they talked about their lives, pursuits, likes, and dislikes. They even laughed together when they talked of the funny things that Emmie had done as a baby, how one year Paige had hidden Easter eggs every day for two months because it kept Emmie busy while she studied.

Settling into the thought of spending time together, Paige began to pick up dishes, and Maddox helped her.

"You have a nice place here."

"It isn't glamorous, and it's small. But it's enough for Emmie and me. Ava, the doctor I work for, and my friend Carly's dad, who's a banker, helped us get it."

"How long ago did you move to Camden Grove?"

Paige poured Emmie's leftover water into the sink. "Back in June, thanks to Ava's job offer."

"How'd you get to know her?" He stopped up the sink and began to run dishwater.

"She and I worked together for a short time in Nashville. There was a big office scandal there. The one you read about. Our main doctor was a crook who tried to pull the two of us into his trouble." Paige squirted dish detergent into the water.

"After Ava left the office, he fired me and started making some false accusations that left both Ava and me hanging in the balance. She ended up contacting me, and we helped each other keep our reputations intact. Then, she offered me a job here. I jumped at the chance."

Maddox shut off the water and began to wash. "Sounds like a good friend."

"You have no idea. I was down to the last straw when Ava showed up. Emmie and I were holed up in this dive of an apartment in Nashville trying to stay out of the way of the parking lot drug deals and gang fights." Paige lowered a couple of plates into the sink, and her fingers touched his beneath the water.

Before she could pull away, he cradled her hand, and she looked up. A bleak expression clouded his eyes. "I'm so sorry you've been alone, Paige. That you had to deal with that. I wish I'd known."

His eyes lingered on hers. His voice resonated through her as he laced his fingers in hers. "I want to help. I've come here for you and Emmie. What can I do?"

That question, the one question no one had ever asked her, struck with the impact of a train. Her knee-jerk reaction only days ago would have been to push him away, to do things all on her own. But now?

"You don't have to answer that right this second. I want you to take time to think about it." He stepped closer. His squared jaw, stubbled and rough, tightened.

She swallowed hard. Her pulse throbbed in her throat as he reached a hand to her face and drew a long, wet line the length of her jaw to her cheek, traced with his eyes the straight path to her lips.

She breathed now, in sync with him, savoring the feel of his touch. He moved closer, within intimate reach. And all the things that mattered moments ago faded like watercolors in rain. Nothing really mattered in that moment—the lost years, the loneliness, the anger—nothing.

When he leaned down, her heart came alive, ached with the luxury of being so close to him, with the recognition that, though she was scared, she truly wanted him there.

It was a millisecond frozen in time, the brush of his lips. Not even a kiss, really, just the hint of something to come.

Then, a voice.

Emmie's voice.

The same one that had barely cried out when she was born broke the silence in the room, bridled the ripeness of the moment.

"Mommy?" she called from the living room. "Can I have. A cookie. For dessert?"

The deflated moment brought Paige back to the room, back to reality. Flustered at first, she wet her lips and stepped back, smoothing the front of her dress—the dress she'd chosen for him—in nervous strokes.

"We should probably finish up here. In fact, I-I can get this later."

"I'm sorry, Paige."

"No. It's okay." She wiped her face with a dishtowel. "It's just that . . . I have some studying to do. I should get to that." She nodded, handing him the towel.

After drying his hands, she followed him into the living room to say his goodnights to Emmie, who disputed his leaving the best she could, wanted him to stay for a sleepover like the other kids at school had. Paige's face turned warm at the thought. She listened as he explained to Emmie how he'd love to spend more time with her, but that he needed to go.

Disappointed, she offered him hugs. "I love you, Daddy."

He pulled her a little tighter, his chin resting on her shoulder. Before letting her go, he whispered something in her ear that caused a wide, eye-squinting smile, then stood, nodded at Paige, and stepped out the door.

She followed him onto the porch and closed the door behind her. When he reached his Jeep, she couldn't let him leave without an answer to a question that had been needling her the whole evening. "Maddox?"

He turned back.

"You kept that buckeye all these years. Why?"

He smiled. "When I left, I didn't stop loving you, Paige. Besides, I told you I'd keep it with me forever. Maybe a little luck is what led me here." He winked, turned, and got into his Jeep.

She didn't breathe again until he drove out of sight.

Chapter Seventeen

Maddox

On his way back to the Mulligans', Maddox squeezed the steering wheel as reawakening feelings for Paige steamrolled through his mind. His attraction to her burrowed a path deep in his heart, not the surface attraction his comrades had found in their weekend rendezvous, not even the feelings he'd left behind in Treemont all those years ago. Now it was much more.

He'd watched as she'd done all the little things for Emmie—served her at the dinner table, walked with her on the old train tracks, laughed at Emmie's jokes. Something about being with both of them, watching and talking and eating together, had kindled something beyond what he knew from years ago. He wondered if this is what falling in love with them both felt like?

Then his thoughts went to the moment they'd just had alone. Her touch left him more alive than ever, opened a place for possibilities.

But that didn't come at an easy price.

That evening, he sat in the Blue Room staring at the reenlistment contract. By coming to Camden Grove, he'd walked into the labyrinth, and now, for every direction he turned, he faced a blank wall, backtracking, winding, becoming more confused with each bend.

Behind one turn, he'd see Stokes and Tigler, all the guys, their stupid jokes and ribbing, the missions they'd served together. Those memories pointed him to an easy out. Just sign the papers and go back to work. Pay child support and go on with life. He was a Marine.

At the next turn, he'd find the Colonel with a pen in hand, compelling him to re-up with stories about legacy and responsibility. He reeled away from those thoughts, angry at the confusion they added, resentful that he'd even let them in.

But, for every serpentine corner he rounded, for every blind alley he backtracked, he'd get a flash of Emmie calling him Daddy or the memory of touching Paige that afternoon—thoughts that brought him to the heart of his dilemma.

Still dressed and caught in a roil of thoughts, he fell asleep sometime after midnight, lost in the maze.

Chapter Eighteen

Paige

After Maddox had left, Paige sat at the kitchen table, flipping aimlessly through the pages of an anatomy text. Studying had been hopeless. Her thoughts wavered between Maddox and Emmie, between what she once wanted more than anything, and what she now feared just as much. Why had he kept that misshapen little buckeye? She knew what he'd said, and it rocked her to the core.

She'd spent her whole adult life shielding herself and Emmie inside a bubble, thickened by a determination to depend on no one. Then, just when she'd begun to gain traction on her own terms, Maddox came into the picture, and suddenly, that bubble began spinning out of control, waiting to burst in the whirlwind.

She rose from the table and pulled a cup from the cabinet. Turning on the tap for a drink, her fingers lingered on the pewter fixtures he'd touched only hours earlier, as if by staying there, they could somehow absorb some errant spark he'd left behind. She wanted to feel it. Wanted that kiss by the sink now more than she'd ever wanted anything before. But did she dare hope for it?

After a last sip of water, she put the cup in the sink and turned out the lights. Climbing into bed would be easy that night. Going to sleep, not so much.

Chapter Nineteen

Maddox

Sunlight streaming through the curtains and brightening the room to an arctic blue served as a wake-up call to Maddox the next morning. That and the sound of rattling outside his window.

When he peeled back the sheers, he saw Hugh with a strand of Christmas lights wrapped around his shoulders, precariously ascending a ladder, Glenna gesturing and fretting a few feet below.

Through the window, Maddox could hear her muffled objections about Hugh's determination to hang the lights. He waved at the man, telling him to wait, that he'd come help, but before he finished mouthing the words, the ladder scrapped away from the wall, tipping back, and Hugh tumbled to the ground in a heap of lights, the ladder landing on top of him.

Maddox ran down the stairs two at a time. The crisp, cold grass nipped at his bare feet as he rounded the corner of the house to find Glenna kneeling beside her husband, the old man moaning in pain.

"Hugh, are you alright?" Maddox pulled the ladder away.

Blood, saturating a patch of his silvery hair, now streamed down his forehead. Glenna stripped off the apron she had on and wiped at the wound. "Oh, Hugh, I told you to leave those lights alone." She turned to Maddox. "He's bleeding something fierce."

"Here. Put pressure on it here." Maddox took Glenna's hand in his and pressed the apron against the cut. "It's a head wound, so it'll bleed heavy at first."

Hugh huffed and groaned.

"Should we call the ambulance?" Glenna gathered the apron as she held it on the wound.

"No, for heaven's sake, Glenna," Hugh snapped. "I'm not dyin'. It's just a lit'l rut in me head."

Maddox pressed on the old man's legs and arms to assess him further. "Doesn't seem to be any broken bones."

"No," the old man grunted some more. "I'm not broken, other than me pride."

"Are you sure we don't need to call the ambulance?" Glenna persisted.

"I'm not going anywhere in a meat wagon."

Maddox spoke up. "Looks like you'll definitely need some stitches." He looked at Glenna. "I can drive you two over to the doctor's office. Just keep pressure on that cut while I go grab my shoes."

"Oh, thank you, dear." She shifted to get into a better position. "You go on."

Maddox took the steps back to the bedroom again two by two, slipped his shoes on, and grabbed his jacket and keys.

When they arrived at the clinic, the front lot was empty. Paige unlocked the door just as he opened it from the outside. He hadn't taken time to wash up, so when he stepped into the waiting room, her eyes went wide at the sight of blood on his hands and shirt. "What happened? Are you alright?"

"It's not me. It's Hugh Mulligan. He fell from a ladder a few minutes ago, and it came down on top of him, cut his head. He'll need some stitches. Is the doctor in?"

"She should be here any minute." A rush of breeze ruffled the plant on the waiting room table as the back door to the clinic opened. "That's her now. Do you need help bringing him in?"

"I've got it."

"I'll tell Ava you're here."

By the time Maddox and Glenna got Hugh inside, Paige had already propped open all the entry doors.

Dr. Fenn followed them into the exam room with a suture kit and washed her hands as they helped him onto the table. "Hello there, Mr. Mulligan. You've started your day off with a bang, haven't you?" Sympathy colored her smile.

"I don't think it's that deep." He nodded. "But it was either come see ye or go in an ambulance." He leaned toward Ava. "Between the two of us, I'd rather be hauled in a hearse. Just cut to the chase is me philosophy."

Ava smiled. "Well, let's hope nobody will need either today." As Hugh sat in a slump, she peeled the saturated apron from his sticky scalp and revealed the cut. "You definitely need a few stitches, and you happen to be in luck, Mr. Mulligan. I can tie off a mean knot." She looked at Maddox. "If you'll help him lie back on the table, I'll get a few things ready. Mrs. Mulligan, I'll give you these gauze pads, and I'll need you to keep some pressure on that cut for me for a bit."

Hugh grunted in response as Maddox and Glenna eased him into a lying position.

As she opened the suture kit and readied a shot of Lidocaine, the doctor looked at Maddox. "I've had the pleasure now of meeting both of the Mulligans, but I don't think we've crossed paths yet. I'm Ava Fenn."

"Doctor." He nodded. "Name's Maddox Granger."

"Yes, Paige mentioned that you'd come into town." She peeled back the packaged tools and placed them on a tray. "Emmie and my fiancé's son, Toby, have become good friends since she moved here." She stepped to the side of the table where Maddox stood.

"So I've heard." Maddox shifted. "I met, uh, Logan, isn't it? And his brother—can't remember his name—a few days ago at the barbeque place."

"No surprise you'd find him and Wyatt both there. They like to torment each other over a good plate of ribs."

Hugh grunted again as Glenna pressed his wound with the gauze. The doctor turned her attention, but before she started work, she nodded toward the door. "Maddox, you're welcome to wash that blood off your hands. The bathroom's just down the hall and on the left. With Mrs. Mulligan's help, I think we can get this sewing project underway and have you all back home shortly."

He turned to Glenna. "I'll be right outside if you need me."

"Thank you, honey. You're an angel."

As Maddox closed the door behind him, Paige rounded the counter and looked again at his bloody hands. "Come with me."

Slipping off his jacket, he set it on the counter and followed her to the end of the hall. She turned on the water and waited for it to warm. "You're just set on becoming the community hero, aren't you? Gabby at the Creamery and now Hugh at the bed-and-breakfast. You stay around here much longer, and they'll dedicate the next parade in your honor."

He shifted on his feet, agitated at the notion. "Nobody's hero here."

Paige nodded for him to come closer. "Water's warm." She stepped aside as he scrubbed his hands.

Looking into the mirror, he saw Paige staring at him over his shoulder. The scrubbing slowed, the water trickled down the drain in a slow stream. She turned away, pulling some towels from the dispenser.

When he shut off the water, she handed him the towels and leaned back against the wall. "This morning, when we were eating breakfast, Emmie asked about last night. She wanted to know why you had to leave so soon."

"Maybe I should've told her."

"Told her what?"

He moved closer. Then closer still until he could feel the space between them build with a charge. "That I had to leave, or I was going to kiss her mother until she asked me to stop."

Paige's lips parted.

Maybe she was stunned, maybe angry, maybe both. He didn't want to take time to analyze every angle or prepare for every outcome. He didn't need years of military training to know there'd be repercussions. It didn't matter. He wanted to kiss her.

And so he did. Slowly, urgently, gently, and passionately. Then he stopped.

The tops of her fingers brushed across the stubble of his chin as he lifted her hand to kiss her wrist, then her palm, never releasing her eyes from his.

Touching her again left him keenly aware of how hollow he'd been without her. "I want to see you again. Your place? Tonight?"

She nodded.

Down the hall, the exam room door opened, and they heard the muffled voices of the doctor and Glenna.

Maddox claimed his last kiss on the tips of her fingers and left.

Chapter Twenty

Paige

After Maddox and the Mulligans left the office, Paige attempted to refocus on her work.

"You're not fooling anyone, you know." Ava stood at the counter, grinning.

Paige shook her head. "I'm sorry."

"For what? Not being able to concentrate after that beautiful man came walking in here?"

Paige smirked. "I didn't know you had a thing for bleeding octogenarians?"

"You know exactly who I'm talking about, and he's nowhere near geriatric. He's very attractive." Ava plopped herself in a desk chair opposite Paige. "So, how'd it go this weekend?"

"Emmie fell in love with him the second she saw him, we ate ice cream at Dawson's, he met us at church yesterday, we went for a walk, and she invited him home with us for dinner afterward."

"Wow. He's getting some face time, then. That's good, right?"

Paige exhaled. "What if this is all just another disaster waiting to happen?"

Ava rolled her chair closer. "Paige, this man has searched for you, traveled to find you and Emmie. He could have stayed away, but he didn't. I'm pretty sure Mr. and Mrs. Mulligan think he had something to do with the hanging of the moon. Surely he can't be all that bad." She propped her elbows on the desk. "Look, you know my history. I haven't had the best of luck with men until Logan came along. But it doesn't take luck to recognize when people have a good heart. Seems like I'm seeing the signs. That's all I'm saying."

Paige turned and looked out the window. "He's coming over again tonight."

"Maybe that's a good thing. A little more time together doesn't make a lifelong commitment." Ava rose from the chair and rounded the desk to call in her next patient. "Unless, of course, it does." She winked.

Before Maddox arrived that night, Paige already had Emmie ready for bed. Dressed in her footed pajamas, Emmie wiggled with excitement as Paige brushed her teeth. "Can I stay up? And see Daddy?"

"You can stay up long enough to say hello. Then it's off to bed." Paige's habit of tucking Emmie in early had been her practice since she started back to school. The quiet time for study was necessary and good for both of them, even though Emmie took a while to go to sleep.

When the knock came at the door, squeals and claps erupted from the bathroom. Paige barely got the toothpaste rinsed from the little pink toothbrush before Emmie trotted toward the front door.

Despite the rush of crisper November air, Maddox barely crossed the threshold as Emmie threw her arms around him in a euphoric hug.

"Hello there, Em." He closed the door and kneeled beside her. "Looks like you're all ready for bed."

"Mommy makes me. Go to bed early."

"I see." Maddox smiled. "I bet she wants you to be rested and ready for your day tomorrow."

"Can I stay up? For a while longer? Pleeeeease, Mommy?" Emmie begged.

"You can look at your book for a while, but it's definitely time to wind down."

"Can Daddy tuck? Me in?" Emmie's eyes widened.

Maddox looked at Paige. "If you'd rather I didn't, it's okay."

Paige pressed her lips into a thin line. "Have you asked him?"

Emmie turned to Maddox, sheer delight shining in her eyes. "Will you tuck? Me in, Daddy?"

His smile broadened as he nodded at Paige. "I'd like that."

Emmie took him by the hand and led him down the hall to her room. Paige heard her giggle as she went through the nighttime routine of telling her stuffed animals goodnight, fluffing her pillow, and settling into bed.

From the hallway, she could hear Emmie ask, "Will you? Read to me?"

Maddox hesitated. "What do you like to read?"

"Rhymes. I like rhymes." Paige knew that, by now, Emmie was reaching for her favorite book—the one the hospital had given her when she was born. They'd read it so many times that several of the pages had come loose from the binding.

She could hear Maddox's muffled response. "Okay. I'm not sure how good a job I'll do, but we'll try it."

"You'll be. Great, Daddy." Emmie's voice echoed through the hall.

As Maddox began to read about an old woman with a broom sweeping cobwebs from the moon, Paige slid down the wall. She sat, knees bent to her chest, listening to the voice of the man she'd lost so long ago, now reading to her baby the same singsong book she had grown to recite from memory. Reading to *their* baby.

How many times she'd ached to hear that voice, reading, singing, talking, whispering. To hear this man saying all the goodnight things to his daughter. They were the sounds she continued to fight falling in love with . . . despite knowing that was exactly what she was becoming powerless to do.

You'll be. Great, Daddy. The faith of a child sometimes rubs off.

Chapter Twenty-one

Maddox

Maddox read the small book, not once but twice, then claimed his goodnight hug, closed the bedroom door, and stepped into the living room with his hands in his pockets. Emmie had just told him again that she loved him, and he found himself easily telling her the same. The night before, when she'd said those words, he whispered into her ear that he loved her too. Not because he didn't want to say it out loud, but because he wanted to spare Paige the worry it may cause. But now, he wanted to say it where everyone could hear it because, from the very core of his heart, it was the truth.

When he came into the living room, Paige, waiting on the couch, had her legs folded and feet beneath her. She had a different look about her, like the cogs in her mind—those trying to figure out how to accept his arrival—had finally stopped grinding. The casual sportswear she wore hugged her slender figure, and for the first time, made her appear relaxed.

"I've never read a book to a kid before."

"She talked you into the usual two times through, didn't she?"

He grinned and nodded.

"You're good with her. I'll admit, I didn't expect that."

He laughed. "Thanks for the vote of confidence. I suppose you're not the only one, though." He sat down on the couch beside her. "The guys back at Lejeune—when they heard the story and found out I was coming here, they thought it was a pretty crazy move."

"And what did you think?"

He paused. She didn't know about his three months of waiting and wondering, about the turmoil of deciding to come.

"Look, Paige, I don't know where this is going, but I want to be totally honest with you. Too much of what we lost was based on keeping secrets. I don't want that on our shoulders anymore."

"What do you mean?" Concern clouded her face.

"At first, I didn't even know what to do with the thought of being a father." He stopped as abruptly as he started, ran an impatient hand through his hair. "I was scared, Paige. The truth is I didn't start looking for you until three weeks ago."

"But I thought you started looking for us when you found out."

"It took a while for me to . . . move on that."

He watched her jaw go slack as the realization of his words settled in. "You waited? After you found out, . . . you waited?"

"I'm sorry, Paige. It was a shock. Look, I wanted to tell you because I want to be honest, to start off on the right foot."

She pulled her legs from beneath her and hugged them to her chest.

Before he could go any further, his phone vibrated in his pocket, and the timing couldn't have been worse.

He glanced at the screen, then at Paige. "I'm sorry. I have to take this."

When he stepped into the kitchen to take the call, he hoped it would be quick and for a reason other than what he suspected, but a call out of North Carolina didn't likely mean anything good

When he returned to Paige, she was standing at the window, looking out.

"When do you leave?" she asked, her voice monotone. "That's what the call was about, wasn't it?"

He paused. "Yeah. I'm on NTM—forty-eight hours' notice to move. I'll be leaving soon. Really soon."

"Figures." She continued to stare out the window.

Then, it all came out of nowhere—the thought, the words, the urgency. "Why don't you and Emmie come with me? I'm up for re-enlistment, but re-upping means I'd have access to benefits that could help with Emmie. We could find a place for you two to live close to base. I could help take care of you both. And maybe we could start over."

Paige shook her head, still facing the glass. "Stop. Stop, Maddox. We don't need to be taken care of. We've got a life here and a place where we finally belong. I'm not about to uproot us again to take a chance on something like . . . whatever this is."

"But we could make it work. I know we could."

"This is *not* what I'm about, Maddox." She faced him. "I told you a long time ago that the military wasn't the life for me. When my uncle Robert came home in a casket, that was all the confirmation I needed."

Maddox bowed his head. "I'm sorry about your uncle. But we could make this work, at least until I finish up this enlistment and decide what's next." He knew he was only trying to buy time and doing a feeble job of it, and he had no time to reinforce his argument before Emmie burst into the room.

"Mommy! Mommy! Where's my. Backpack? I have something. For Daddy!"

"Emmie, you're supposed to be in bed." Paige turned away, dabbing at her eyes.

"Mommy. That paper."

"What, honey? What paper?"

Emmie started jumping up and down. "The paper. About the 'tillion."

"We'll talk about it later. Go on back to bed."

"But Mommy, no. I have to. Get the paper. For Daddy."

Paige pinched the bridge of her nose as Emmie ran to find her backpack.

She came back into the living room, the bag slapping against her legs with every step. "It's in here."

"No." An expression of understanding crossed Paige's face. "It's not in your backpack."

"Where *is* it?"

"I put it away in the drawer. I thought we might ask Logan if he could take you."

Emmie frowned. "It's not. For Logan. It's for Daddy."

"What's she talking about?" Maddox asked.

"A 'tillion. A daddy-daughter. Mommy-son dance." Emmie dropped the backpack and clapped her hands. "I want you. To go." She turned and shuffled into the kitchen. Paige closed her eyes and shook her head as if it would clear her mind.

When Emmie returned a few seconds later, she waved a flyer in the air. "Here, Daddy. This is for you. They're giving us. A dance. Will you take me?"

Rubbing his jaw, Maddox took the paper from Emmie. The wrinkled flyer promised the event of the year: a cotillion, something he'd never before imagined attending. "I guess we'll have to wait and see, Em."

"But. You'll take me. Won't you?" She wasn't giving up easily.

Paige interrupted. "Sweetheart, he may not be here when they have the dance. Maybe they'd be okay with a mommy and daughter coming together."

"That's not. The same." She turned to Maddox. "You'll come. And take me. I know you will." Emmie smiled and nodded.

Paige tried to put her off. "Let's just see if maybe Logan can take you. Okay?"

In that moment, Maddox saw the hope in Emmie's eyes evaporate like a mist against heat. "I don't want. To go. With Logan."

Maddox cleared his throat. "I'll be here."

Whipping around, Paige glared at him as if he'd just promised a trip to the moon.

Emmie clapped her hands again and hugged his neck. With little convincing from Paige, she then scuttled off down the hall, as excited as if she'd been given an early Christmas.

After the door to Emmie's room closed, Paige snapped, "You can't do that. You can't just promise her you'll be here when you and I both know you won't be."

"I can at least try."

"Trying doesn't mean coming through. And she'll be here waiting for you with her heart broken." Paige folded her arms. "You just don't get it. She, least of all, deserves to be left waiting. I can't even understand you." She then threw up her hands in frustration. "You ride into town and re-open every wound I've tried to let heal over the last six years, then tell me you weren't so sure that being a father was a line printed on your fortune cookie." The words spewed out like a toxin. "And now you're dragging Emmie into it?"

"Paige—"

"Stop. I'm just getting started. I'm sorry that after all this time of being AWOL from our lives, it took you three months to figure out that you just might want to find out what an amazing daughter you have. Three months may not seem long to you, but I'll tell you it can be an eternity if you're waiting with your last shred of hope."

"That's not fair, Paige."

"Don't *even* talk to me about what's fair. I'm sorry that you're delusional enough to think that what's fair to you matters to me, because it doesn't. I've got someone else to think about now—someone who doesn't deserve having to wait for you or wonder if you'll ever come back." She crossed to the door and opened it. "Just do us all a favor, Maddox, and go back to your life."

He brushed past her without looking back, ripping from himself all the hope he'd brought with him as he walked out the door.

Chapter Twenty-two

Paige

The energy drained from her like sands from an hourglass. She didn't even know what had just happened. All the anger and bitterness had bubbled up like acid, burning her to the core, and Maddox took the brunt of it. Her shoulders shook as she silently cried. With her face buried in her hands, she didn't hear or see Emmie come into the room.

"Mommy? He'll be back."

Paige drew in a gasp, wiped her tears, and stepped to Emmie. "Honey, you should be asleep."

"Why are you? Crying?"

Paige knew she couldn't hide what Emmie had already seen. She pulled her to the couch, and they sat down. "Sometimes adults just cry, baby."

Emmie reached up and tucked a strand of hair behind Paige's ear. "Do you? Miss Daddy?"

Paige had always promised to be honest with Emmie, but she didn't know how to answer her question. The truth was, she'd missed Maddox for six years. Had thought of him nearly every day and couldn't help but see him when she looked into Emmie's eyes. And yes, she missed him. She missed the fact that he'd made her feel different from the very first moment she'd met him. That when she got to know him, he uncovered parts of her she didn't even know existed. And when she lost him, part of her vanished with him.

When she couldn't respond, Emmie spoke for her. "Mommy. You should. Be happy. He's coming back."

"Oh, sweetheart. I *am* happy because of you. Your daddy gave me you, and you're all I'll ever need." That was the first time she'd ever broken her promise to be truthful to Emmie. And as she hugged her little girl, she knew that Emmie knew it too.

Chapter Twenty-three

Maddox

Paige's words rang in his ears as he pulled into the Mulligans' drive.

She'll be waiting for you with a broken heart.

Go back to your life.

The temperature had dropped a good bit since sunset, and though he'd always preferred the warmer days of summer, Maddox didn't hunch beneath the collar of his jacket or regret the coming winter. Instead, he welcomed the chill as if it offered him a deadened place where he could untangle the Gordian knot that the summer months had given him.

Those few white Christmas lights Hugh had strung before his fall gave the antique house a soft glow. The rest of the lights still sat on the porch in their tote.

As he opened the door and stepped inside, he found Glenna sitting in the parlor, reading in the easy chair by the lamp.

"You're back earlier than I expected."

"Yeah," Maddox said softly. "How's Hugh?"

"Stubborn as a barnyard mule. Won't take a painkiller, even though his cut's achy. Heaven help him, and me, too, 'cause I love him, the old Irish coot."

Maddox gave a weak smile. "I think I'll turn in." He stepped toward the stairs, then hesitated. "How long do you think it'll take to get the rest of your lights up?"

"Oh, I'm not worried about that anymore. We'll just have to bow out of the Christmas Tour this year."

"No need. I'll get to work on it in the morning." Before he turned again to go to his room, he added. "I'll be leaving soon, but I'll do that before I go."

Glenna frowned. "Aww, I hate to see you go. You've been such good company and quite a help to us around here. You haven't seemed like a tenant at all. More like a grandson."

Maddox smiled at Glenna and rubbed at the shadow on his chin. "Glad to help."

As he climbed the stairs to the Blue Room, he took solace that at least someone accepted his offer.

Early the next morning, Maddox dismissed the thought of further sleep when he awoke from his restless night, just as unsettled as he'd been the day before. Convinced that he was better off busy, he dressed, went downstairs, and slipped out the conservatory door to begin work on hanging the remaining lights on the garden side of the house.

An hour later, Maddox heard Hugh shuffling across the stone pad toward him.

"How're you feeling?" Maddox called from the ladder.

The old man chuckled. "Like me head's been split open."

"Sounds reasonable." Maddox tugged at a strand of lights, balled into a massive tangle.

"Breakfast is ready. Ye should give this job a rest and get something to eat."

"You and Glenna go ahead. I think I'll finish up here."

Hugh paused, tilted his head. "What're you doing here, lad?"

"Trying to untangle these lights. I should be finished before long." Maddox stretched the knotted strand.

"No, son." The man shook his head. "Why'd ye come all the way to the Grove? It weren't to help an old Irishman with his holiday decoratin'."

Maddox stopped and held the lights slack.

"Y' say ye came looking for the woman and your daughter, and ye found 'em. But far as I can see, it's you be the one needin' findin'."

Maddox descended the ladder and dropped the lights into a tote. "I did come to find them."

"For what purpose, then?"

Maddox shook his head. "I wanted to show that I claimed responsibility. To meet Emmie and tell Paige I was willing to help."

"Is that it?" Hugh's tone was clipped and stern.

"I asked her to come back with me . . . but she won't. I thought maybe that was an answer."

Hugh squinted his eyes. "Of course she's not goin' back with ye. She's got a head on her shoulders. I'm bettin' she's fought to get where she is. Ye don't single parent without puttin' up a fight. She'd not give it up at the snap o' yer finger."

"So, what do I do with that?" Maddox looked away. "I'm leaving here in hours, and in the next few weeks, I've got to either sign re-up or discharge papers." He put his hands on his hips. "Before I came here, I thought I already knew which I'd be signing."

"And now ye don't?"

"This trip hasn't made it that simple." He ran a hand through his hair. "Since I was two, I knew I'd be a Marine. My father laid out a clear path. It's all I've known." He knew it wasn't an answer to the question.

Hugh swatted at the air impatiently. "That's an age-old story, doin' what other people expect of ye. Is it in *yer* heart?"

Hugh's question punctuated the moment with weight.

"If it is, then do it with yer whole heart. But, if it's not, then know that ye've served your country, even yer father. And consider what it means to serve another purpose. There's no shame in that."

Maddox shook his head. "I've got a team of men. We depend on each other."

"Well, then, seems to me ye've got to decide whose face will haunt ye more when the head's on the pillow at night."

Hugh's hard truth jarred Maddox's thoughts. He turned back to the tote, picked up the string of lights, and began tugging and stretching again. "It's not that easy. I can't just drop everything and walk away."

When he turned back around, Hugh was gone, and he was alone, still untangling.

An hour later, Maddox pulled the last string of lights from the tote. When his phone rang, he draped them over a bush and bristled at the North Carolina number flashing on the screen.

Within a two-minute call, Maddox had orders to cut his leave even shorter. The NTM window had been cut by a day, which meant he needed to return that night, get his gear in check, and report for mission briefing the next morning at 06:00 hours.

As he ended the call, Maddox tilted his head to take in the morning sun. It had warmed the air, but had done little to illuminate his mind with solutions. And now this.

He looked at his watch. The drive back to Camp Lejeune would take ten hours with gas stops. He hurriedly hung the string of lights over the last bush, stacked the empty Christmas totes, and went inside.

Glenna, putting away the breakfast dishes, sighed. "You've saved us a world of work, honey. We surely do appreciate it."

He nodded, then looked at Hugh sitting at the small breakfast table a few feet away. In front of him, piles of documents lay in assorted stacks, and binders with hole-punched pages sat open with sticky notes attached in random places. "What's all this?"

"It's family history. Look here." The old man motioned for him to come closer. His aged fingers, drawn and arthritic, pointed to a particular book with a sticky note. On the paper was the name

Granger. "I knew I'd run across your name in some searches. I tend to write down the meanings of names when I find one snaking through a family line of mine. See here? Yer name Granger? It means *homesteader*." He chuckled. "Funny how names mean something."

"And what does Mulligan mean?" Maddox asked.

"A do-over. A second chance." He looked from under his hooded bushy eyebrows. "Got that second chance when I was ambushed in the Congo, and I've had a few others in me time. Can't count on too many of 'em to come yer way, though. No, not at all. Anyway, I thought ye might be interested to know that lit'l tidbit."

Hugh's prod didn't go unprocessed. Maddox tucked it away. "I just got a call from base. I'll be leaving this morning. Got orders to return." He nodded toward the garden beyond the conservatory. "When it comes time to take those lights down, if the neighborhood kids can't help, I'm sure you could call one of the lawn-mowing businesses in town. They usually welcome work this time of year."

"Don't you worry. We won't be getting back up on that ladder anytime soon." Glenna rounded the kitchen island. "We're surely sorry to see you go. You'll have to come back as soon as you can."

Maddox glanced at his watch again. "If you don't mind figuring what I owe you, I'll settle up when I come down to leave."

Glenna waved him upstairs. "You go get cleaned up, and we'll talk before you go."

Maddox made quick work of getting ready and packing his things. From a zipped side pocket, he pulled a thick mailer envelope he'd prepared before leaving Camp Lejeune. Paige would be at work by now and Emmie at school, but he knew he couldn't leave without taking care of a few things first.

With his bag packed, he returned downstairs, where Glenna and Hugh had moved to the front parlor. He set his seabag on the floor in the same spot it had lain the first day he'd stepped into the Mulligans' home.

Glenna smiled as she handed him the bill for his stay.

"This can't be nearly what I owe you."

Hugh waved his hand. "We've talked about it. Ye carted me off to the doctor's office. Ye've decorated the place for Christmas. We've been spared a lot of worry with all ye've done to help us." He pointed to the bill in Maddox's hand. "That'll be more'n sufficient to cover the expenses."

"I—"

"Don't argue now." Glenna's sternest voice could still warm a cold heart.

Pulling a few bills from his wallet, Maddox slipped in an extra and extended his hand. Glenna threw her arms around him, patting his back. "You stay safe, and stop in when you come back to the Grove."

"Yes, it shouldn't be hard to find yer way back." Hugh nodded and offered a firm shake of the hand.

"Yes, sir." Maddox pulled the bag to his shoulder and slipped out the door quickly.

He never did like goodbyes.

As he drove away, the old Victorian house in the rearview mirror looked even bigger. He wondered if Hugh was right, or if it would be impossible to find his way back.

Maddox was closest to Camden Grove Elementary and made that his first stop, as the clinic was on his way out of town. With another look at his watch, he decided if he made a quick stop at both, he should have enough time to fuel up and still leave enough of a cushion reasonably to return to base by his deadline.

He pulled into the bus parking lane and jogged toward the building. At the door, a sign directed him to buzz the front office from a call box at the right of the entry. At least they were security conscious. He pushed the button, and soon the friendly voice of a woman chimed in on the other end. "Can I help you?"

"Yes, I'm here to see Emmie Westerfield."

"And what's your name, sir?"

"Maddox Granger." He paused. "I'm her father." The words hadn't come out loudly enough for them not to sound peculiar.

The call box went silent. After a few seconds, the voice replied, "I'm sorry, sir, but there's no Maddox Granger on Emerson's contact profile."

He rubbed the back of his neck. "Yeah, her mom wouldn't have made that change yet. Look, I just need to see her for a couple of minutes."

"I'm sorry, sir, but it's against policy for us to let anyone come in who isn't listed on the student's contact profile."

"I understand it's a security concern." He persisted, this time nearly begging the woman on the other end of the call box. "It'll just be for a couple of minutes. Somebody can be right there with us. I'm just leaving town and wanted to say goodbye."

The voice on the other end sounded more impatient this time. "I'm sorry, sir, but I can't make an exception. You can have her mother come down to the office and sign the change-of-profile form, and then we can let you in. Otherwise, I can't."

Maddox dropped his head against the brick wall. "Okay, can I at least leave something for her? You can take it right here at the door, and then I'll leave." Maddox thrust his hand into his pocket.

The woman on the other end paused. "Let me check with our principal."

Maddox tapped his fist against the side of the building and looked at his watch. Finally, the door buzzed, and a woman with a short, blunt haircut and sharp features opened the door with the security officer by her side. "Hello, Mr. Granger. My name is Mrs. Forester. I'm the principal here. Is there something we can help you with?" She missed her calling as a drill sergeant, Maddox thought. Her flinty voice demanded attention.

Maddox glanced at the officer. Then, he put something in the woman's hand.

As the officer stretched to look over her shoulder, the principal held it between thumb and index finger, looking at it as if it were the most curious thing she'd ever seen. "You want to give her this?"

"Yes, I do." He was insistent.

"Is she supposed to know what it is or what it's for?"

Maddox thought for a moment. "Tell her it's one of a kind just like her and that I wanted her to have it for luck." He turned and started to leave, then looked back. "Oh, and Mrs. Forester, tell her I'll be back to get it on the night of the cotillion."

He turned and jogged across the lot without looking back, not fully knowing why he'd just made that promise for the second time in as many days.

At the clinic, the waiting room seats were full. Paige looked up from the office window as Maddox came inside.

As he approached the window, she stood and quickly came closer. "What're you doing here?"

"I came to see you for a few minutes."

She lowered her voice. "I'm working. You shouldn't be here."

Maddox shifted. "I wouldn't have, but I'm on my way out of town."

Paige's expression remained stone cold. She nodded to her right. "Come into the office."

As he came through the door, he could see the wall Paige had once constructed between them now reassembled in her expression. She folded her arms. "Back to base, I guess?"

"On assignment. I don't know where yet." He paused. "And I couldn't tell you even if I did."

She shook her head. "And what am I supposed to tell Emmie now?"

"I tried to stop by the school to see her, to at least say goodbye to her, but they wouldn't let me in."

"That's their job—not to let in strangers." Her eyes bored into his.

Maddox tried to ignore the cut, took his fiftieth glance at his watch that morning. "I wish I weren't leaving here like this, but I have to go." He pulled the thick envelope from inside his jacket and set it on the counter in front of her.

She eyed it. "What's this?"

"It's something for you and Emmie. Put it away for now and open it when you have some time to yourself to read what's inside. I really have to go. I'll be in touch. But before I leave, you asked me what you were supposed to tell Emmie? Tell her I love her."

Seconds later, he pulled back onto Main Street, headed out of town, knowing he'd break speed limits on the way back to Camp Lejeune. Being on such a tight rope would cost him some worry, but that wasn't the cost he was worried about.

Chapter Twenty-four

Paige

When Maddox left, Paige stared at the envelope. She wanted to open it, but before she could decide either way, a patient in the waiting room tapped at the receptionist's window to hand over a clipboard full of paperwork. She quickly slipped the envelope into her desk drawer and stepped to the window, almost relieved that it would have to wait until later.

The morning kept her busy. Ever conscious of what was inside the desk, Paige finally took a lunch break a few minutes early and went to her car for privacy.

After closing the car door, she took a deep breath and unsealed the envelope. She first pulled out a stapled set of papers. The top page was a Designation of Beneficiary Form. Her gasp broke the silence when she read her name listed on the form as primary benefactor on Maddox's life insurance policy. Emmie was a secondary. She then turned the envelope upside down. A bundle of hundred-dollar bills slid out along with a blue piece of stationery.

For a moment, Paige sat stunned. Only a few months ago, she'd come to Camden Grove to start over, and though she had the hope of a new life for her and her daughter when she arrived, she was still a long way from real security. She'd never dreamed of Maddox considering her and Emmie's future by doing something like this.

She unfolded the stationery and began to read.

Dear Paige,

Finding the right words to say everything I've wanted to say has never been my strong suit. I can't undo the mistakes of the past, the countless times I wasn't there for you and Emmie. For that, I'm truly sorry.

Despite everything, I do know that Emmie has had the very best mother. I know this because I learned something about you a long time ago. As soon as we met, I could tell you were independent, capable, and smart. Any girl who could sell a buckeye to an Ohioan has some true savvy.

Tears welled in Paige's eyes as a smile crept along her lips. She leaned back against the headrest and drew in a stuttered breath. With the contents of the envelope in her lap, she gathered her emotions and continued reading.

I also now know for certain that the girl I found under that tree a few years back had a much stronger heart than most. But even a strong heart is breakable. I'm afraid I've been responsible for breaking yours.

Recently, I took a step to ensure some small measure of security for you and Emmie. As it turns out, the military has a good life insurance plan. Enclosed you'll find the form declaring you both as beneficiaries on my policy should anything happen. While it can never make up for lost time, it's my simple attempt to provide some support for the future.

Please understand that this decision doesn't come with any expectations or conditions. I don't suggest that a man can buy forgiveness. It's much harder won than that. I only hope that doing something right for you and Emmie, after such a terrible wrong, will lead to a truce.

You know, six years ago, when you tossed a good luck charm to the boy under that tree, he didn't know he'd grow up to be a man who wondered just how lucky he'd have been if he'd stayed by your side.

Always yours,
Maddox

Paige's hand trembled as she refolded the letter and placed it back in the envelope. For the rest of her lunch break, she sat in her car and cried.

During a short afternoon lull, Ava sat down in the chair opposite Paige's desk and stated the obvious. "If you were any more distracted, I'd worry that you'd use the plugin as a pencil sharpener. What's going on, Paige?"

She shook off the stupor and looked up. "I'm sure you could guess."

"Probably, but what specifically?"

Paige drew in a deep breath. She decided not to go into too much detail. "Maddox stopped by the office this morning. He left to go back to base. Said he had an assignment."

Ava nodded. "So, did you two leave on good terms?"

"Not exactly." She paused. "I told him he should've never come to Camden Grove."

"Do you feel like that's fair?"

Paige looked harshly at Ava. "What is it with people and being fair? I think that's more than fair, considering."

"Considering what?" Ava pressed on as calmly as still water.

"How about for six lost years?" She shook her head.

"Paige, I'm your friend, and because of that, I'm going to be honest with you right now."

She cut her eyes toward Ava.

"Since Maddox came into town, you've talked a lot about those years you struggled."

She could feel herself stiffen.

Ava raised her hands in defense. "I'm not saying you don't have cause to be hurt or angry. I can't imagine the struggles you've had, but a few months back, when I visited the woman in that beat-up little apartment taking care of her little girl the best she could, I didn't see someone confined by a feeling of entitlement."

"What's that supposed to mean?" Heat rose up Paige's neck.

"It means I saw this grit in you to move forward." Ava continued. "If I'm honest, that's one reason I wanted you to come to Camden Grove. I knew you'd be a perfect match for helping me get this practice up and going."

Ava laced her fingers beneath her chin. "Paige, sometimes people deserve to feel hurt or be angry. They've earned the right to restitution, maybe when it's not even possible, but the minute they *feel* entitled, they have to be careful that it doesn't enslave them." She grasped Paige's hands. "All I'm saying is that you have so many more places to go with your life—so many more things to do with Emmie—if you're not shackled by the past."

Before Paige could gather her thoughts enough to respond, she heard the back door to the office open. The voices of Toby, Emmie, and Logan prattled down the hall alongside the clicking of Toby's service dog's feet against the tile floor.

Ava lowered her voice. "I'm your friend. That's why I'll always call you out when I feel you should look through a different set of lenses. I hope you'll do the same for me."

Coco rounded the corner for his usual doggie treat from Paige as Emmie called out, "Mommy, Mommy! Look what. I've got."

"What's that, baby?" Paige raised her eyes from Coco to see Emmie's open hand in front of her. When she saw it, she couldn't bring herself to speak.

Lying in Emmie's palm was Maddox's buckeye.

"Is something wrong, Paige?" Ava asked.

"No, I just—where did you get that, Emmie?"

She closed her fingers around the buckeye and held it to her heart. "Mrs. Forester said. Daddy left it. At school. For me."

Something inside Paige ached at the sight of it, at the memories behind that little seed.

"Mommy, we have. To buy tickets. For the 'tillion."

"Yeah," Toby set a flyer on the desk in front of Ava as Coco stood wagging his tail. "Will you go with me, Ava?"

Logan rounded the counter and leaned in to kiss Ava on the forehead. "Looks like I'm losing my girl to a seven-year-old Casanova."

"What's a Casanova?" Toby wrinkled his nose.

Ava squeezed the boy and whispered, "A handsome young man, and just between you and me, I think your dad's jealous." She winked.

"So does that mean you'll go?" he asked.

"Of course, I'd be honored to go with you to the cotillion."

Emmie's grin widened as Paige's heart sank. "I can't wait. To tell Daddy."

Paige pulled a treat out of her desk for Coco and forced a smile. "We'll have to talk a little more about that, sweetheart. I don't think Maddox will make it, but maybe we could get Logan to take you." She turned to Logan with desperate eyes, hoping Emmie wouldn't show her stubbornness. "Would you be willing to help us with that?"

She could tell by his expression that Logan picked up on her plea. "Of course." He kneeled down by Emmie. "Miss Emerson Westerfield, would you do me the honor of being my date to the cotillion?"

Emmie's grin faded, but then she smiled again. "Okay, but only if. My daddy. Doesn't come."

Ava chuckled. "You'd better get in line, Mister. This little girl's talking options."

Paige reached over to shut off her computer. "We should probably get going, Emmie. I've got to study tonight, and I bet you have homework."

Ava arched an eyebrow. "Before you go, are we good?"

Paige nodded, though Ava's challenge still stung.

"Good. Oh"—she punctuated the counter with her finger—"remember, this weekend, you, Carly, Jessie, and I are driving over to Hartley and meeting Lydia for dress fittings."

Paige nodded and slipped her jacket over her shoulders. "I'll be there."

Emmie hugged Toby goodbye and turned to Logan. "My daddy will. Come to. The 'tillion." She held out her hand with the buckeye. "It's for luck. He said. It's one. Of a kind. Like me."

Logan nodded as Paige exchanged glances with Ava. "I can't argue with that, sweet pea."

As she shouldered her purse strap, Paige felt more than the weight of a bag on her shoulders. Calling for Emmie, she said, "Come on, baby. Let's get on home."

Chapter Twenty-five

Maddox

For three days, Maddox forced thoughts of Paige and Emmie from his mind. Once he got his mission directives and sat in flight with his team, he knew distractions like those would cost lives if he didn't get his head in the game.

As the C-130 Hercules soared through the darkened skies, its cargo hold filled with the elite team, the tension inside the aircraft was palpable, each Raider mentally prepping for his part in the mission. The team members, clad in their specialized gear, checked and rechecked their parachutes, ensuring everything was in order. As the red light inside the aircraft signaled their proximity to the drop zone, the anticipation intensified.

"You okay, man?" Stokes sat geared up next to Maddox.

He nodded.

"Not good enough, my friend. Remember who you're talking to." All the men had dubbed Stokes the mentalist—that is, when they weren't jabbing at him, calling him the mental case. "You went to see your kid last week, right?"

Maddox nodded.

"So that's what's eating you. Let me guess. You're still in love with her mother."

Maddox cut him a hard look.

"Don't take a mind-reader to figure that out. You've not said two words since you got back."

"Look, I'm trying to get my head on this mission."

"Yep." Stokes's gave an exaggerated nod. "Best place for you to be right now, but you know as well as I do that if something's rocking your boat, we're all going in the water. I'm just trying to clear things up before we start paddling."

Maddox shook his head. Stokes always called things as he saw them. It's what made him a good Raider. He was quick to assess and mitigate, and his team never had to wonder what he was thinking.

"I'm considering calling it quits." Maddox confided.

Stokes obviously knew to what Maddox was referring and nodded again. "Tell me something new."

"I'm serious."

"Look, we all think about that every time we take on another mission, every time we jump out of another plane, every time we're put in the crosshairs. It's part of the job. But here's the deal. Bad as I hate to admit it, Barber was right. Before we hit that ground, we'd better be asking if we're in it 100 and a half."

Maddox's mind went back to the moment he'd first heard those words. When he and his team were in the thick of CQB training, learning the ins and outs of battle in close quarters, their trainer,

Gunnery Sergeant Max Barber, screamed it—"a hundred and a half"—over and over in their ears for weeks. "A hundred percent'll getcha killed," he'd yell. It took a hundred and a half to bring you home. And nobody wanted to do any more than that.

In the few private moments the team had over those torturous weeks, they found entertainment in mocking Sergeant Barber and his pet phrase, but when it came down to it, he was telling the truth they all knew.

Stokes piped up. "If you've not got that in you, man, it's too little for you, and it's too little for the rest of us. No shame, just truth."

With a soft punch to the chest, Stokes repeated, "Hundred and a half, man." Then he went to re-check his equipment for probably the fifth time.

Those words simmered in Maddox's mind until Tigler gave the final nod and the rear cargo door opened, revealing the vast expanse of foreign airspace below.

The rushing wind filled the cabin, stirring the adrenaline like a thick soup. Maddox patted at his chest pocket, maybe to make doubly sure he hadn't left anything behind, maybe to reaffirm his new good luck charm. Tucked inside were the photo of him with Paige and—folded several times—the wrinkled flyer for an elementary school cotillion.

In turn, they approached the open hatch, and one by one, ran into the void. Just ahead of Maddox, Stokes turned and gripped him by his harness. He yelled, "Hundred and a half. Before you hit the ground." He then ran full speed into the darkness.

Maddox took a deep breath, then followed.

In that fleeting moment, suspended between the plane and the earth, he resolved to do more than his hundred and a half because he had more to do than just get home.

Despite the nighttime seventy-degree temperature, the heat index from the previous day spilled into the darkened streets of the small foreign port city like a blanket cast over a feverish child. Maddox and his team scanned the nooks and shadows from their perch behind an abandoned car, waiting for the right moment.

The hotel, splotched with graffiti, sat in the distance, a concrete abuse to the ground space it occupied. Two paint-chipped tuk-tuks, the three-wheeled taxis of a couple of barely employable street vendors, were parked to the side of the building waiting for daylight and a patron moneyed enough to use their services.

Days earlier, the other side of the village had seen violence when a group of gunmen attacked a dilapidated government building, taking two Americans and a Briton hostage. They were among the few who survived the attack, but for what form of torture, no one had the desire to conjure a notion.

The men had special ties to lawmakers aimed at bringing order to a city that extremists were otherwise committed to upending. They were more valuable as an example than a simple kill. Execution would have been too easy.

As a result, a week later, Maddox and his men sat in the darkness behind a car, readying themselves to reclaim the hostages and expedite them to an extraction team.

They'd studied the facade of the building, along with the typical construction layout in the briefing. They knew that the clay brick took on a hue somewhere between pink and terracotta in the daylight hours. But in the darkness, the dirty grayish color of the structure made sure identification more difficult.

As Maddox studied the landscape from a distance, the only identifying feature that rang true was the lay of the multitude of wires overhead. The web of lines had no semblance of order. They reminded him of the Christmas lights he'd tried to untangle at the Mulligans' days earlier. He pushed the thought from his mind and confirmed with a more focused scan that they'd found the abandoned hotel they were looking for.

Before the first hints of morning movement, Stokes gave the sign, and the crew spread in the darkness. From the back entrance of the abandoned building, he led his men with the stealth of a faint breeze as they scaled a set of stairs along the outside wall.

At the second floor, they stopped and waited until he felt confident about moving further. As they reached the third-floor landing, Stokes's hand signals directed a risky move into the main hall. Exposed to their enemies.

Maddox first lay on the concrete floor and eased a hand-held micro camera around the corner to see if the hall was clear. He breathed only after he found it empty.

The men then rounded the corner, silent as cats. The doors along the hallway had been torn from their hinges. They passed each room with guns readied against their shoulders.

At the end of the hall, one room stood behind a closed door. That was likely their target. When they were within thirty feet of the room, a burst of gunfire rang out behind them, spattering against the concrete, raining down on them in chunks.

Maddox yelled as the men dived to the floor, landing in rooms on either side of the hall.

They scuttled on their bellies to find cover. Maddox caught a visual on all his team. All still moving.

No one had come from the room with the closed door. That meant one of three things: either the gunman behind them had been left to guard the entry alone, or whoever was in that room sat waiting to pick them off. Or both.

The guard would expect low fire.

He'd have to be eliminated first and fast.

Maddox kept crouched as he darted to the edge of the door and pulled a dusty chair from a heap on the floor. He propped the chair against the door frame and, with the speed of a snake, whipped around the edge. Bullets spattered in a rainstorm of gunfire. Then silence. And the thump of someone falling.

The men waited for another count of five, then Stokes and Tigler covered their backs while the rest of the team rounded the corner and rammed the door of the closed room.

They claimed the space in a wave.

The three dignitaries sat tied to chairs, wild-eyed, bruised, and disheveled.

When Maddox tore the gag from the face of the Briton, the man struggled to talk, his voice raspy and dry. He began to chatter in a crazed stream. "They're coming back. We have to leave. They're taking us to another compound. We have to leave now!"

When they'd freed the other men, Stokes sent Bailey and Lamberg out to clear their exit and put Pate, Gillings, and Tigler with the three hostages to cover them while he and Maddox closed the back.

As they exited the building, the eastern sky began to turn from charcoal to a lighter shade of violet. Maddox knew, when he heard the car round the corner two hundred yards to the south, that it couldn't be good news.

Stokes ordered the men in front and those covering the hostages to go on while he and Maddox stayed behind to divert attention. They took cover behind the tuk-tuks.

Picking up speed at a hundred yards, a gunman leaned out the passenger window as Maddox and Stokes opened fire.

Maddox's heart rammed against his chest as the militant fell from the car window into the street, and the glass from the windshield shattered into a web.

At thirty yards, the car careened toward the tuk-tuks—Stokes and Maddox still firing full force.

Twenty.

Ten.

He never felt the impact of the bullet or of the car. Instead, he simply saw Paige and Emmie sitting across from him in the ice cream shop—Emmie smiling with her creamy mustache and white nose. Paige cleaning up the mess he'd made trying to help.

Chapter Twenty-six

Paige

Four of the five women stood outside the bay window of the Bridal Boutique, scrutinizing the dress on display. The tulle, draped from end to end, created the illusion that marriage in this dress was a fairy tale in satin.

Paige, not really in the mood to critique, listened as the others chattered.

Once inside, the attendant took them all to the dressing area, where a line of wedding dresses in Ava's size was already hanging on the pre-selected stand. Another empty rack stood next to it for those she rejected.

Also in the room hung a selection of dusty- and powder-blue bridesmaids' dresses of varying sizes and shades for the other four women to try.

Carly, the first to jump in, began expeditiously sliding the dresses from one side of the rack to the next. "Okay, ya'll, I'm calling any gown with an asymmetric neckline." She pulled a dress from the rack, held it up to herself, and spun around toward Ava. "It has that Greek goddess vibe, don't you think?"

"The chiffon is nice too," Jessie commented without looking. "Are you sure you're alright with us choosing our own style, Ava?" She ruffled through the selections at a casual pace. "I thought brides made all the choices for their weddings."

"Yeah, but Ava doesn't speak Bride-zilla." Carly yanked another one from the rack.

"No, I'd like you to have something you could wear more than once if you wanted. The powder- or dusty-blue colors. That's my only request."

Lydia held a dress up to her shoulders. "I've found my first try-on. What about you, Paige? What style are you looking for?"

Half-heartedly glancing at a couple of dresses, Paige shrugged her shoulders, her attention focused elsewhere.

Ava peeked around the rack. "You still with us?"

She raised her eyes. "Yeah, sorry. Guess my mind's in other places today."

"Wouldn't be in the same place as that hunk of military property, would it?" Carly grinned and tossed her purse on a white leather sofa.

Paige didn't answer. Instead, she plopped down in a chair and sighed.

Carly draped the dress over her arm and sat down next to her. "You okay? I was just kidding."

Paige shook her head. "Do you ever get worked up because somebody says they'll do something? And even though you don't expect they will, something inside you clicks, and you expect the unexpected?"

Carly's eyes clouded with confusion. "That sounds like a lot of expectation gone wild."

"I know I'm not making sense." She frowned. "Maddox said he'd be in touch. Not that I imagined he would after how I treated him, but—"

"But you expected him to," Carly stated the obvious. "When were you supposed to hear from him?"

Ava, Jessie, and Lydia left the racks and sat down on the ottoman in front of Paige.

"He didn't say. I don't even know where he is or if he's able to. When he left town, he just said he would." Paige shook her head. "You were right, Ava. I didn't give him much of a chance."

Leaning closer, Ava took Paige's hand. "Maybe he just hasn't been able to call for some legitimate reason."

Lydia smiled. "If I've learned one thing about men since being married to Wyatt Carter, it's that they have a different sense of time than women. And, yes, that's a sweeping generalization, but either way, he's bound to be in touch soon."

Paige scanned the faces of her friends as they tried to paint the best scenario. She sighed. "I'm sorry, Ava. I've wasted enough time and energy worrying about Maddox Granger." Gripping the arms of the chair, she stood. "Today's your day. Let's buy some dresses."

The four women eyed her skeptically.

"What? Why are you looking at me like that? Isn't that what we do, perk up when we get to spend money?"

Carly shrugged. "Now she's talking my language."

"That's right, sister." Jessie bounced up from the ottoman, pulling Lydia with her.

Ava squeezed Paige's hand. "You're not raining on my parade if you want to talk more about this."

"Thanks, but I'm ready for a distraction." Paige smiled and faced the racks as the store attendant returned from the front showroom. "How's it going, ladies? See anything you like?"

"Yes, I know exactly which one I want to try." Paige shored up her resolve and headed for the racks.

In another two hours, Ava was still searching. "How did y'all find dresses so fast?"

"Could it be we're more decisive than you?" Carly prodded.

"I just want something simple." She threw a layer of crinoline fluff hanging about her waist into the air. "Not frou-frou."

Before she wilted under the weight, the attendant came back from the showroom with a dress in her size that had just been delivered. "This isn't as fancy as the others, but I thought you might like to see it."

Ava took the gown into the fitting room while Lydia went to the bathroom and Carly and Jessie plopped on the couch across from Paige.

"So, how's Emmie doing with Maddox leaving?" Jessie asked.

Paige shrugged her shoulders. "I don't think she understands. She's still expecting him to come take her to the cotillion the school's having in a few weeks."

Carly propped her feet on an ottoman and turned to Jessie. "By the way, partner, I got a call from the PTA coordinator. We're supposed to shoot that event." She then turned back to Paige. "Maybe he *will* come. Where did you say he's stationed?"

"North Carolina. Camp Lejeune."

"And he's there now?"

"I don't know where he is. He's in Special Ops, and he said they had a mission."

"That explains why he's not calling you. I don't think I'd give up on the guy just yet."

"When's the cotillion?" Jessie asked.

"Next month."

"That's plenty of time," Carly said. "Don't chase away possibility with negative thought. You never know. He could be the one. The perfect one."

Lydia returned from the bathroom and pulled out her lipstick just as the door to the bride's dressing room opened.

When Ava stepped onto the mirror-encased platform, all eyes were on her. The sheath-style dress, fitted at the waist, fell to the floor below her hips with a subtle, unassuming flair. The modest train was embedded with daydream tulle and embroidered in soft florals, the same as the sleeves attached to the square neckline of the bodice. Everything about the dress spoke simple elegance.

All the girls, at first speechless, came alive with incessant chattering. Paige then rounded the ottoman and made the statement everyone else was thinking. "The perfect one."

The dress was truly perfect for Ava, but it wasn't only the dress she was thinking about when she said those words.

In her heart, she knew that—just like Carly said—Maddox was the perfect one for her.

Now, how did she accept and act on that truth?

Chapter Twenty-seven

Maddox

The ceiling came into focus in waves, just like the nausea. Then the pain in his right arm forced Maddox into consciousness. He could hear a clicking to his side.

Willing his head to turn, he fought off the queasiness to see a stout-looking nurse tapping away at a keyboard near his bedside. When she noticed him, she patted his head with a wet cloth and shushed with gestures and muffled words his efforts to speak.

Then, the pain closed in, and the room turned black.

When he came to again, light streamed at an angle along the bare wall from a window with no blind. A blue curtain hung from a bending rail encircling half of his bed—the folds of the fabric like bars on a jail cell until they came into focus.

As his vision cleared, he became more aware of the pain in his right side, began to recognize all the telltale signs: the hard bed, the mobile IV cart, a small rolling tray. They all confirmed his kindling awareness of where he was, that he was injured . . . but alive.

Just as he tried to raise his head, a new nurse, petite with a friendly face, came into the room with a chart in hand.

"Ah, you are awake." A midwestern accent rolled off her tongue. "We need to get you up soon."

Maddox tried to speak, but his throat was a sheet of sandpaper and glue. She wet his lips and mouth with a swab, and the words came in a whisper. "Where am I?"

"Landstuhl Regional."

Landstuhl was the largest American hospital outside the United States, providing medical care for military personnel across the European theater. During his various deployments to the Middle East, he'd been a part of evacuating too many Marines to the German-based hospital. When the nurse said Landstuhl, he knew then that his team had transported him to the extraction point and medevac'd him there. His injury must've required attention that a field facility couldn't handle.

"What happened?"

"You've been shot, and your right side was injured from the impact of something else."

A memory flashed in Maddox's mind: the tuk-tuk. He was taking cover behind one of the tuk-tuks when the car rammed into him and Stokes.

Stokes.

He tried to speak again, but the words came out in a brush of weak air. He ran his tongue over his lips. "Anybody else—?"

"Shh. No. You only. But I hear that your unit's well."

Relief washed through him as the nurse administered something in the IV.

"How long—?"

"You've been here two days." The nurse had obviously answered those questions many times before.

Two days.

"I have to get up." His vision went black with pain when he tried to raise himself upright.

The nurse pushed him back to the bed with little effort. "You have to rest now. Someone from your medical team will speak to you soon."

As the IV meds worked into his bloodstream, his fight against the fog again became useless. His last thoughts, before the tidal wave of darkness, settled on Paige and Emmie half a world away in Camden Grove.

"Wake up." The stout nurse's round face hovered over him as the darkness diminished from the edges of his sight. Beyond the window, the sky was black.

"You should drink something. The longer you stay in bed, the harder it will be."

"What day is it?"

"Sunday." The nurse raised the bed to a reclining position.

Maddox couldn't tell if it had been minutes, hours, or days since he'd last opened his eyes. "Where's the doctor?" His breathing escalated as the nurse steadied him. Stabbing pain shot through his shoulder, and he moaned.

"You were asleep when he came through earlier. The doctor should be in tomorrow."

She pushed a wheeled tray against the bed and raised the plate cover to reveal a cup of brown liquid. The very smell of it sickened him. He turned away. "Later."

"Maybe this will be motivation for your recovery." The nurse set the bent photo he'd had tucked in his pocket on the tray in front of him. Beside it, she laid the unfolded cotillion announcement. "One of the trauma nurses found these inside your cammies after the doctors cut them off. Pretty girl, there." She nodded.

Maddox eyed the photo. Something stirred inside his chest that he'd locked up before the mission. "Yes, she is."

The nurse poured a cup of water from a plastic pitcher and left Maddox with the admonition that he should try to drink the broth soon.

As he sat in the empty room, he held the picture for a long time, wondering if Paige would ever be part of his reality again.

The night passed with an occasional visit from an orderly to check vitals. He welcomed the interruptions as he tried to push away uninvited images from his head: the wild-eyed Briton tied to the chair in the battered hotel; the car careening toward him and Stokes as they crouched behind the tuk-tuks; and, unexpectedly, the smug grin of his CO handing Maddox his reenlistment forms.

With each new image, a wave of dread rolled over him, and, with each new wave, he looked at the picture of Paige and drew in the comfort he felt when he'd kissed her. He thought of Emmie's face when he said he'd take her to the cotillion. She had nothing but joy in her eyes. Those were the threads that stitched up his wounds.

In the dim light spilling from a beeping machine, he gritted through the pain, propped himself up, and pulled the tray close. After his breathing settled, he stirred the broth with a plastic spoon from the tray, the brown liquid now cold with a filmy skin.

He drank in slow, determined sips.

He was going back home.

Back to Camden Grove.

Chapter Twenty-eight

Paige

The week of Thanksgiving, Ava invited Paige and Emmie for a holiday dinner at Wyatt and Lydia's cabin in Hartley. Despite knowing she and Emmie would enjoy visiting with the Carters, Paige first declined the invitation. Imposing on a family during the holidays wasn't something she leaned into, but Ava and Logan insisted that the gathering would include others besides immediate family.

Jessie had invited Carly since her parents were taking a trip to Europe. And Carly's boyfriend Jex was coming in from Atlanta to meet all her friends, so he'd be there too. Ava finally convinced her to come when she said that Logan had also asked a couple of his buddies—a contractor friend named Dakota and Wiggs, the owner of the local barbecue place—to join them. Truthfully,

Paige didn't want to be alone for Thanksgiving, and she wanted something to look forward to for Emmie as much as herself.

By the time they arrived at the Carters' cabin, conversations rumbled in every corner, and someone had set up a folding table to extend the dining space.

Paige placed a pecan pie in the middle of the dessert buffet and handed a box of vanilla bean ice cream to Ava to put in the freezer. As she hung their coats on a pegged hall rack, she gazed around the room at people chatting and laughing as festive music played in the background.

She'd never been to a family gathering this big before. Her holiday dinners growing up were low-key affairs, just another day for her dad to indulge in an online poker match and her mother to start early-bird shopping. Not the warm and cozy occasion for gratitude or holiday spirit.

At first, taking care not to draw much attention, Paige found a chair in a corner and watched Emmie trot off to play with Toby. Every few minutes, someone would pass by and say hello, or one of her friends would throw conversational bait her way. She mostly kept to the role of a quiet observer, though.

Once dinner was ready with all the trimmings, the smells wafted through the house in an invisible, mouthwatering cloud. Lydia and Wyatt's mom, Margaret, said they'd begun preparing the meal early that morning. Logan's friend, Wiggs, had brought in a spread of sides fresh from his restaurant, and with all the other guests adding desserts, the table looked like a Norman Rockwell painting.

Wyatt pointed his dad, Gus, to the head of the table, and Margaret sat by his side. Once everyone else found their seats, Gus spoke. "I'm glad we could all meet here at Wyatt and Lydia's to have this meal together. It's not every day you get to spend time with your friends and family around such a fine table of food." He reached for Margaret's hand. "Before we say grace and dig in, most of you know my lovely wife's affection for tradition. Our custom's always been to start our Thanksgiving meal by sharing one thing that's happened this year that makes us grateful. Anybody like to start?"

Logan cleared his throat. "I can definitely say I'm thankful I found Ava, and that she helped me get my favorite little man, there, the medical attention he needed." He winked at Toby.

"That's two things," Wyatt teased, "and I'm gonna tell you a third you should be thankful for. Don't forget, Carly and I had to give you two a good hard nudge in each other's direction. You should throw some love across the table here, too."

The guests laughed as Carly lifted her glass in agreement. "Here, here. And I wouldn't have had the idea for that blind-date photo shoot had it not been for this man." She laced her arm through Jex's. "I think everybody's met my new favorite guy by now, and since we're sharing gratitude, I'm grateful he taught me a some of his photography tricks."

Jex clinked glasses with Carly. "I got the better part of that deal, so for that I'm thankful. And coming to Camden Grove, meeting all of you. It's been a real treat. I'm excited to tell my family up in Chicago about your Southern hospitality."

"Yep, no shortage of that when Mom's around." Wyatt chimed in, a mischievous glint in his eye. "Just be warned now. She won't be satisfied if you get up from the table without gaining a few extra pounds or leave the house without a plate of leftovers."

Margaret swatted a hand at Wyatt. "You know you love it."

"No denying."

When the laughter died down, Wyatt took Lydia's hand and said, "While I'm still allowed to talk, I'll tell you now that I'm sharing my gratitude after dinner when my tummy is full of what I'm thankful for." More laughter erupted.

Comments continued, turn-by-turn, circling the table until it came to Emmie seated across from Paige. "I'm grateful. My daddy found. My mommy and me."

The table went quiet until Paige interceded. "And we moved to Camden Grove. That's made me grateful."

Others fell in line with their input until Logan's contractor friend Dakota offered the last comment. Seeming a bit awkward, he spoke gratitude, but not necessarily for anything about the past year. He simply thanked the Carters for the invitation to dinner. Afterward, Gus said grace, dishes were passed, and the buzz of conversation resumed. No judgment, no afterthoughts, just laughter, compliments on the food, pleases, and thank yous.

As she listened to the chatter, Paige began to understand that no matter what Emmie had said, those around the table accepted her. *That*, she thought, was something to be thankful for.

***

Everyone scattered to various pockets of the cabin's large front room after consuming too much dinner and clearing the mountain of dishes. Emmie and Toby played with Coco and Lydia and Wyatt's golden retriever Milo by the fireplace as the adults talked and the TV played the customary football game—the sort of setting Paige always imagined of a close family.

Watching Emmie laugh and enjoy the people surrounding her left Paige with a keen longing for those kinds of genuine connections.

Ava sat down beside Paige on the couch after sliding from under Logan's arm and coming across the room. "A thousand miles away again? You're getting into a nasty habit of that."

Paige smiled. "This family . . . It's nice to be here."

"Yeah, they're pretty great." She scanned the room. "We'll both be hosting get-togethers like this someday—kids, grandkids, friends all sitting around a Thanksgiving dinner, talking about the good things."

Paige sat aimlessly tracing patterns with her finger on the velour couch cushion.

"You seemed a little uneasy with what Emmie said earlier," Ava prodded.

"That obvious?"

Ava pressed her lips into a thin line and nodded.

"I've been doing this alone for so long, I guess I'd forgotten what it feels like to be part of a family." She watched as Emmie played with Coco. "She's always happy, but right now, I see pure joy in her eyes."

Toby and Emmie then engaged Coco in a tug of war with his chew toy.

"What have I kept from her, Ava? Have I denied her the chance for things like this because I haven't wanted to need anybody? Because I pushed Maddox away?"

"Paige, what you and I see in this family is the result of two people opening their hearts to each other a few decades ago." Ava gestured toward Gus and Margaret, holding hands across the room. "A product of trust, something I'm honestly just beginning to understand myself. I don't know where that starts, but I do know it takes us asking ourselves if we have the courage to take the first steps. So, maybe you shouldn't question what you've denied Emmie, but what you've withheld from yourself."

Paige thought about Ava's words, wondered if she still had the ability to trust.

Before their conversation continued, Carly and Jessie plopped down on either side of them.

"What are you two over here communing about?" Carly cocked her head.

Ava shrugged. "Oh, life, liberty, pursuing happiness."

"Then you guys are constitutionally too serious."

Ava nodded toward Jex, leaned against one of the cabin's wooden columns, chatting with the guys. "Jex seems like a great ."

"He really is. I'm glad he got to come into town to meet all my friends."

"Is he staying for long?"

"No, quick trip. I'm planning to go to Atlanta for Christmas, though, so I'll be able to spend time with him then."

"She's got her guy. You've got yours." Jessie nudged Ava. "Let's talk about that beautiful man over there talking to Logan and Jex—the one I'm gonna marry someday."

Ava followed Jessie's gaze. "Dakota?"

"Um-hm. He is yummy."

"Nice guy." Ava shrugged. "Logan's been friends with him for quite a while. I don't know much about him other than he's kind of shy, distant at times."

"And how do you know this intriguing fact?" Carly settled into her seat, tucking her feet beneath her.

"He's been around when I've been over at Logan's a few times. Like I said, sweet guy, but every time I ask him something about himself, he gives me a generic answer. Almost evasive."

"Maybe he's a spy." Jessie widened her eyes playfully.

"Not the Double-O-Seven type."

"Or maybe he's just conflicted, like Paige, here," Carly said.

"Then heaven help us if there's more than one like me in the room at a time."

"Truer words, my friend, truer words." Carly poked her in the side.

When the giggling stopped, Jessie leaned in and whispered, "Hey girls, word has it Lydia and Wyatt have some news to share."

"Is this *the* news?" Ava arched an eyebrow.

"Looks like we're about to see."

The four of them watched as Wyatt pulled Lydia to the center of the room and dinged a spoon on the side of a glass. "Ladies and gents, we've assembled you here today for a reason."

"And it's not for the afternoon football," Lydia added.

"Here I thought we'd go into our annual Thanksgiving coma in front of that big screen." Logan lowered the TV volume and tossed the remote to the ottoman.

"Nope." Wyatt shook his head. "Lydia and I wanted to share what we're grateful for this year." He turned to his wife. "Ready, sweetheart?"

She nodded.

Wyatt lifted his glass. "My wife, here, is grateful that I'm going to have to eat my pride and ask this brother of mine if he'll do some remodel work on one of our bedrooms."

Lydia chimed in. "And my husband is grateful that I'm not decorating it to be his 'I'm-in-the-doghouse' room." Everybody laughed. They looked at each other, then Wyatt turned to Logan. "We need it converted into a nursery."

The room erupted with clapping and squeals. Jessie stood to hug her sister as everyone else lined up to share in the excitement. Logan grabbed his brother in a bear hug and kissed Lydia on the cheek. She beamed, accepting pats on her belly and congratulations all around.

Paige glanced at Emmie sitting on the floor by the fireplace, clapping and laughing with the rest of the crowd.

She watched her daughter celebrate with the whole family.

When they returned home that night, Paige put Emmie to bed and ran the tub with steaming hot water. She searched the cabinet for an old bottle of lavender bubble bath—an extravagant office gift from her former employer, the one who'd bilked her out of an honest job months back. She'd packed it with her when she left Nashville because it was the only thing representing luxury and relaxation she'd ever remembered owning.

Once the tub was filled with sweet-scented bubbles, she slipped her robe to the floor and enveloped herself in liquid comfort. Thoughts rambled through her mind in an endless diorama, then settled on the most pivotal event of her life—the night she'd gone with Maddox to the boathouse.

High school graduation had been checked off the list—"Pomp and Circumstance" played, mortarboards tossed, and all the graduates tucked away at their respective parties. Neither she nor Maddox had celebrations on their calendars, though.

The Westerfields found little to commemorate unless it involved gambling or shopping. And Colonel Lewis Granger dictated that he and his wife save their celebrating for the day their son graduated from boot camp, well on his way to a career in the Marines. *That* was cause for celebration, not a piddly high school ceremony.

In the last days of their senior year, neither she nor Maddox spoke much of the coming day when he would leave for boot camp at Parris Island. They'd barely have moved their tassels before the Colonel would cart him off.

In hindsight, Paige understood now that he'd likely realized, even before she or Maddox did, that their friendship was maturing into something more. Something that he couldn't allow. He'd discouraged their time together at every turn, and as a result, sneaking around had become their practice in the weeks leading up to Maddox leaving.

So, reckless as it was, that night, after graduation, they planned a few last hours together. Not with intentions for intimacy, more as a last occasion for solace.

With everybody asleep, Maddox had rolled his dad's car out of the drive and showed up throwing pebbles at Paige's window a few minutes later. When she sneaked with him past the hedge to the curb, her parents had never been the wiser either.

The Grangers' boathouse sat twenty-five miles upstream of the Cumberland River on the reservoir of Old Hickory Lake. She remembered the drive there was quiet. Two naïve kids searching for comfort, Paige thought.

She sighed at that memory as she sank deeper into the tub—allowed others to flow freely now.

Less than a minute into the trip, Maddox reached across the console and laced his fingers with hers. She breathed slowly in an effort to soak in what she'd grown to crave since he first kissed her. When he looked at her through the dim light, they both smiled. From time to time, they glanced at each other as she tried to memorize the sensation of his thumb stroking the back of her hand. It was something she never wanted to forget.

Once at the boathouse, they hiked hand-in-hand through the darkness until they found the path to the dock. Moonlight spilled its glimmer across the water as they drew nearer to the Colonel's cabin cruiser.

Maddox stepped on board first, reaching back for Paige's hand. As she moved from the dock, the boat accepted her weight with a gentle dip and rise. Her stomach floated with the same easy movement.

She'd never been inside a cruiser like this before. Her only experience on the water had been in kayaks and canoes at a summer camp her parents once funded as a rare penance for having spent so much on themselves.

This boat had a cabin equipped with a small kitchenette and dining area and, farther to the back, a double bed.

Maddox searched the cooler and found a couple of soft drinks, then turned the cruiser's stereo system to soft music.

At first, he stood across the petite cabin, watching her.

When she turned and saw him, she asked, "What?"

"I want to remember what you look like right now." He paused. "Beautiful."

Paige laughed. "We should take a picture together—evidence of our rebellious streak."

"Yeah, I agree." He pulled the phone from his pocket and stepped in close to her, encircling her with his arm.

After he snapped the photo, he turned to Paige but didn't let her go. "I'll get a print made before I go on base. Then I can look at you every night before I go to bed." He'd already explained that he'd have no personal phone with him once he arrived for boot camp.

"Why would you want to do that?"

"Do you really have no idea?" He looked into her eyes as if combing her thoughts for an answer. "We've spent the last year together, Paige, learning each other's quirks, finding support in those long walks home. For months now, I've wanted nothing more than to tell you . . ."

"Tell me what?" She prayed his answer would match hers.

He moved closer until his breath warmed her lips. "That I love you." He said it as if those were the easiest words he'd ever spoken.

No longer waiting for validation or approval or the right moment, he lifted his hand to touch her face, traced his fingers along her cheek, and sank them into her hair. Then, without reservation, he pulled her into a soft kiss.

She'd never allowed it to materialize before—the need of him. But now she melted into him, feathery and soft at first. Then more insistent.

They kissed each other like they somehow knew it would be their last.

Paige sat in the bathtub long enough for the water to become tepid, but memories of that night kept her warm.

Once dressed in her nightshirt, she slipped beneath the comforter. Thoughts bombarded her—more memories of the night at the boat dock, the dinner at the Carters', Emmie sharing her gratitude for Maddox. It all came together in concert, pointing her to what she'd wanted all along.

She finally picked up her phone and called Maddox's number. Then she hung up before it rang, dropped her head, and dialed again. This time, she waited.

For every second that passed, she forced herself to stay on the line, but he didn't answer. When the voice mail picked up, she sat silent for a moment, unsure what to say. When she did speak, her message was brief and direct. "It's Paige. Could you call me when you have a minute? I'd like to talk."

That night she waited and hoped, cried and wavered, but he never returned her call. In the early morning hours, she fell asleep with the phone still in her hand.

Chapter Twenty-nine

Maddox

Three weeks later.

For each day that passed, Maddox became more impatient to return to Camden Grove. The days spent in Germany and his subsequent transport back to the Naval Hospital at Camp Lejeune had been an ordeal too long in the making, his recovery more physically and mentally exhausting than any training he'd ever faced.

When he did return to the states, Stokes, Tigler, and the other guys came to see him in the hospital. They gave him the play-by-play of his medevac and their extraction with the dignitaries, then joked around for a while until the jokes ran out.

Before they left, Stokes handed him his phone, dead but wrapped in the charging cord. Maddox had requested he bring it from his locker when he came.

When he retrieved his messages, he never suspected that one voice on the other end would be Paige's.

As the recording played in his ear, he almost called her that second. He even pulled up her number. But, with a moment to think, he knew that hearing from him now, after so much time had passed, would do nothing to convince her they deserved another chance. It had just been an abbreviated repeat of the broken promise six years ago. Waiting was something she'd had to do one too many times. Proving to her he wanted a second chance would take more than an overdue phone call.

When he was released, he learned that the Medical Evaluation Board, or MEB, had kicked his case to the higher-ups, leaving his professional fate to their discretion.

But he'd never imagined his career as a Raider would end quite like this.

The gunshot wound had done enough damage, but when he'd dodged the on-coming car, the side mirror caught the same bullet-riddled arm with the force of a stick of dynamite, ramming him into the concrete building twenty feet away. The impact had severed a motor nerve, causing his medical team to recommend further surgical repair within an eighteen-month window. He would be in recovery for the long haul and, if he was incredibly lucky, could regain full sensation in that arm.

In the time since the incident, he'd known, had even come to grips with the fact that a Raider without full use of his arm couldn't do the job of a Raider at all. He knew, before ever being told, that the ultimate decision of the higher-ups would be a medical discharge. That it would be with full honors now seemed less significant to him.

The mix of emotions that came with that decision left him disbelieving it with the same energy that he accepted it.

He now would leave one team with the wild hope of joining another.

Stokes spoke with him the day he left. Maddox knew why—to do what he'd been trained as a Raider to do: assess volatility. Stokes was a brother who'd built his free time around physical self-improvement and honing strategy, skills, and marksmanship. Not much passed under his discretionary eye without him getting a solid take on the situation.

"How're you doing with all this, man?"

Maddox shrugged. "Glad nobody else got hurt."

"That's not what I mean." He folded his muscled arms. "You okay?"

Maddox thought again about the faces that had played on repeat in his head: the Briton, his CO, Stokes himself. Then his mind went to Paige and Emmie. The right focus, he'd learned, was the best of survival tools. "Yeah, I'm okay."

"When you finish up with all the repair work and are rehabbed, give me a call. I've got a friend into high-end security consultation. I'm sure he could use a dude like you."

Maddox nodded. "Thanks, man. I may do that."

They said little else. Stokes must've assessed and gotten his answer. Maddox loaded the last of his things in his Jeep and bid his friend goodbye. Before he pulled away, Stokes called out, "Granger. A hundred and a half."

Maddox smiled. "A hundred and a half." He'd never meant those words more.

As he pulled past the last gate and put Camp Lejeune in his rearview mirror, he took in a hard, deep breath. He now had some place else to be.

Chapter Thirty

Paige

After the hours had stretched to days, and days to weeks, Paige's small flicker of hope faded. No return calls, no letters in the mail. She'd hoped for too much, a miracle, maybe. Emmie's faith, however, never failed.

In the days between Maddox's leaving and the cotillion, Paige tried to avoid thinking about him and the possibility that he'd never come back to Camden Grove, much less show up for a school party. But Emmie, in her excitement, refused to accept anything but her own reality.

The night before the big event, when Paige told her again that she'd have to go to the cotillion with Logan as her escort, she folded her arms. "You're wrong. Daddy will come."

She then turned and promptly stomped into the other room, Paige letting her go without reproach.

As she sat on the edge of her bed, Paige had no tears to cry. The anger and resentment she once felt had faded away.

Weariness had replaced them both. Weariness for Emmie and all the disappointment she'd face in her lifetime and exhausted by the hole in her own heart.

The next morning, Paige surprised Emmie with a new dress. She'd picked it out from the bargain rack the day she'd gone with Ava and all the girls for the bridal fittings.

"I'll be. A princess." Emmie cooed as she brushed her hand over the ruffled, tulle skirt.

In the hours before the cotillion, Emmie asked every ten minutes if it was time to get ready. When Paige finally relented and helped her into the dress, she stood in front of the bedroom mirror, smiling broadly and admiring herself. Rocking back and forth, her skirt swayed side to side as Paige pinned a stray hair beneath her headband.

"You look beautiful, sweet girl!"

"Thank you, Mommy. When will. Daddy be here?"

Paige sighed, then decided not to put a damper on the night. "Logan will take you over to the school, and then if your daddy makes it, he can bring you back home."

Emmie sashayed to the mirror again. "He will, Mommy. I'm a princess." She swayed back and forth.

Paige put her pain behind a smile. "Yes, baby, you are."

At 4:05 p.m., Logan, Ava, and Toby pulled up in the drive.

Ava stepped out in a flattering blush-colored dress and stood by the car with her phone poised for pictures. Toby got out of the back seat and stood beside her as Logan walked toward the porch.

When Paige and Emmie stepped outside, Ava held up her phone to snap a shot. "Sorry we're a few minutes behind. Logan had to go over to the school with Dakota to set up some work lights and patio heaters for the red carpet." She snapped another picture. "Look at you, Emmie. You're beautiful."

Emmie swished her dress from side to side.

Spiffed up in a sports jacket and tie, Logan kneeled on the sidewalk facing Emmie and presented her with a small, white wrist corsage decked in a blue ribbon to match her dress. "Miss Emmie, you are a sight to behold. May I escort you to a cotillion?"

Ava continued to snap pictures as Emmie slipped her hand into the wrist band and wrapped her arm around his.

"You bet." She grinned and nodded big. "Thank you. Mr. Logan."

Paige rested her hand on her chest. The formalities and little details Ava and Logan had taken to make Emmie's night special warmed her heart.

Just as they got to the end of the walk, Emmie stopped. "Oh, wait! I forgot!" She turned and padded back to the house, past Paige, and toward the door.

"What did you forget, Emmie?"

Ignoring her mother, she disappeared inside. When she came back out, Paige repeated her question as Emmie walked past her toward the car.

"This." The little girl smiled.

Logan's brow wrinkled in confusion as Emmie approached. "Whatcha got there?"

"My buckeye. It's for luck. My daddy's coming. To get it."

Paige's heart constricted with the weight of Emmie's expectations, but she didn't have the words or energy to dishearten her with the truth. Instead, she waved again as Logan buckled her in the car.

Toby slid in back with her as Ava turned to Paige. "We're stopping in town to get a quick bite before we go on to the school. Why don't you come over later and watch her walk the red carpet?"

"They really make this a big deal, don't they?"

"The event of the year." Ava nodded. "Anyway, you look a little down. Go put on a fun dress and come join the party. I bet Carly and Jessie would be happy to sneak you in on their photographer's pass. You know how they love being naughty."

As Logan and Ava pulled out of the drive with the kids, Paige went back inside. She walked through the empty house into her bedroom, then stepped into her closet. The question whether to go to the school or stay at home and continue to brood didn't take long to answer. After tossing a few dresses from her closet, she chose one she hadn't worn in ages and headed to the shower.

When the phone rang a half-hour later, Paige was just finishing her makeup. A little part of her still hoped for a miracle, wished she could hear Maddox's voice on the other end.

"Hello."

"Is this Paige Westerfield?"

"Yes, speaking."

"This is Glenna Mulligan . . . from the bed-and-breakfast."

"Mrs. Mulligan?"

The woman hesitated. "Yes, I'm sorry to bother you. I hope you don't mind my calling."

"Well . . . of course not, but how did you get my number?"

"Oh, darlin', I use mutual contacts all the time to get other people's numbers. I hope you won't blame Dr. Fenn for sharing your information with me."

"No, that's fine, but what can I do for you, Mrs. Mulligan?"

"Well, we had the unexpected arrival of a rather unusual delivery today at the house. It has Maddox Granger's name on it. I was wondering if you could reach him."

Paige sighed. "I'm sorry, Mrs. Mulligan, I've tried to call him, but I haven't had any luck." Shifting the phone to the other ear, she slipped off her robe and pulled on the dress.

"Well, you're likely to see him before I do. Would you mind stopping by tonight? I could give it to you for safekeeping."

Sliding on her heels, Paige cradled the phone against her shoulder. "But I don't—"

"It would mean the world to us if you came by and visited for a few minutes. Sometimes gets lonesome here after a quiet week."

Paige held her breath for a few seconds, trying to think of a way to decline, but her thoughts went momentarily to her own loneliness. She couldn't say no. Maybe just a quick stop after the cotillion would do. "I'm getting ready to go to a school event for my daughter in just in a few minutes, but—"

"Oh, that would be perfect. Just stop by before you go, and it'll be waiting for you. I'll just leave the package in the conservatory, and you come right on in when you get here. No need to knock. Well, Hugh's calling for me, darlin'. I've got to go, but we'll see you soon."

When the phone clicked, Paige held it in front of her and looked at it, bewildered. She'd have to hurry now to make it to the Mulligans' and back to the school in time. At least the bed-and-breakfast wasn't out of the way.

She put her earrings on as she walked toward the door, and the phone rang again. This time, it was Ava.

"Paige, you've got to see this. It's all too cute for you to miss."

"I'm trying to get there, but I just got a call from Mrs. Mulligan. Did she call you?"

"No. Are she and Mr. Mulligan okay?"

"That's odd. Yes, they're fine. I just have to make a quick stop by her place, but I'll be there as soon as I can."

"Sounds good. They were supposed to start announcing all the couples in a few minutes, but they've had a delay. That should give you time to get here."

"I'm on my way."

Paige pulled her coat from the closet. Before grabbing her keys and purse, a glance in the hallway mirror stopped her. The black, form-fitting dress was simple enough to be Sunday attire and—with the right accessories—elegant enough to wear to a party. She'd bought it at the boutique on the square with one of her first paychecks in Camden Grove. A little splurge just for her. Now, standing in front of the mirror, she wished more than ever that

Maddox was there with her. Dressing up alone somehow seemed pointless.

With the clicking of her heels across the living room floor, she collected her purse and keys, pushed her thoughts of Maddox away, and left for the Mulligans' place.

Chapter Thirty-one

Maddox

The Blue Room was just as he'd left it. The sun, now setting below the hedges, cast the December sky in a blanket of indigos and pinks, causing the room to change shades by the minute.

Though dressing himself in his pants and undershirt had been difficult, he managed. Knowing that in the past, he'd been a part of taking out foreign regimes but now had trouble buttoning his trousers left him frustrated. Frustrated, but not ungrateful. The uniform coat, however, was a different obstacle. Finally, he called Glenna to help.

As she stepped into the room, she clasped her hands in front of her. "Oh, I just love seeing a man in uniform."

"I'm afraid I'm not quite uniformed yet."

"Here." She took the coat in hand and stepped behind him. "You know that's what turned my head when I first met Hugh all those years ago."

"That he was in uniform?" Maddox slipped his right arm into the coat sleeve, wincing as he straightened it.

"Careful, now." She eased the coat up on his arm. "Not when I met him. I saw a picture of him, though. That's how a mutual friend introduced us."

Once Maddox's other arm was positioned, she pulled the coat to his shoulders. "It's not just the uniform. It's what it represents. There's not a soldier I've ever met that's not dedicated and true to something. Those qualities aren't the easiest to find nowadays."

She buttoned the coat as the creases in her eyes deepened with her smile. "I have a feeling they'll not be lost on your young lady friend, either."

When she stepped back, she released a satisfied sigh and smiled. "Now there, you look like you're ready to claim the prize."

"I hope the prize is ready to claim me."

"Don't you worry. I got everything set up just like you asked. She should be here any minute, so Hugh and I are slipping on out to leave you two to yourselves." She patted his face and kissed him on the cheek. "Good luck, dear, but I don't think you'll need it."

Chapter Thirty-two

Paige

The remnants of sunset lay on the western horizon as Paige walked onto the Mulligans' porch. They'd already turned on their Christmas lights, so the glow of the miniature white bulbs embedded in the draping garland along the porch cast a soft and welcoming glow.

The door, unlocked just as Mrs. Mulligan had said, squeaked as it opened. She heard old music coming from farther inside, likely from the Victrola she'd seen in the conservatory weeks earlier. As she eased toward the sound, the house welcomed her with a collection of antique nativity scenes—one on every side table.

A Victorian tree stood against the long windows of the parlor, decorated with lace cones, sachets filled with cedar, and oranges plugged with cloves. The house smelled of Christmas and did something to warm her as she followed the music.

When she stepped through to the kitchen, she expected to see Mr. or Mrs. Mulligan busy at making dinner, but they were nowhere to be seen.

Then, when she rounded the corner of the breakfast room into the conservatory, her breath caught in her throat.

Chapter Thirty-three

Maddox

Something soft and magical happened in the conservatory when twinkling white lights glittered all the way to the far reaches of the garden beyond. From his position and through the tall glass panes, Maddox could see a spotlight in the distance shining on the perpetual sundial Glenna had so fondly introduced weeks ago. The stationary light settled on the dial as if time were now somehow frozen.

When he heard steps behind him and turned back around, she was there.

And suddenly, it was.

Chapter Thirty-four

Paige

She couldn't breathe. Her mind searched for clarity, tried to reconcile dim hopes with the reality that they were coming true. She took one step forward, her heart pounding, then waited.

Soaking in every detail, standing now only a long shadow's length away, she saw a man dressed like a soldier. Like a protector, yet somehow wounded by choices made a long time ago.

At first, words didn't come.

Not from him.

Not from her.

Only the music played, scratchy but somehow exactly right.

She moved toward him again, stopping within reach, her eyes resting on the black sling cradling his arm. "What happened?"

He didn't take his eyes off her. "I made a mistake."

"I don't under—"

"Shhhh." He touched his finger to her lips. "The short version is I wasn't fast enough to get out of the way of my enemy. The shorter version is that I was my own enemy all along."

"Do I ever want to know the details?"

He smiled. "Probably not. Boring story."

She glanced at his arm. "Are you alright? I mean, will you be?"

"I was alright the minute I realized that this was exactly where I wanted to be." His eyes searched hers as he reached to touch her face. A tingling, like the brush of a feather against lips, climbed up her spine as his hand found its place, once again tracing her cheek.

She had no desire to push him away this time. She'd made that mistake one too many times before. Instead, every ounce of reserve she had vanished, second by second. "I didn't think you'd come back."

Finally, she turned her lips toward his hand, kissed it softly as it lingered against her cheek. His calloused skin, rough and edged, bore the physical analogy to their relationship. She drank up every thought of him, all the images in her head somehow cathartically bringing him more completely home to her.

He didn't need any more of an invitation. Pulling his lips to her ear, his voice was now a deep whisper. "I'm here now, and I want to be here forever. Will you let me prove I'm worth the wait?"

Her eyes welled into pools, all the pent-up uncertainty draining from her with his question.

At first, his lips wandered across her cheek, the now-and-then brush of his clean-shaven face, at times, too far away, then achingly close. He pulled back, as if savoring her before melting into something willful, expectant. Then he kissed her. A soft graze. Then, rich and full.

She matched each kiss with a demand of her own, each one healing her a little more.

In that moment, Paige realized that promises sometimes come delayed.

When they stopped and saw each other in all their vulnerabilities, she lay her head on his shoulder, swayed with him to the scratchy music, and looked beyond the glass of the conservatory at a distant spot in the garden. With all her thoughts now lost in him, he held her close under the twinkling Christmas lights until the music stopped. When they looked at each other again, Maddox spoke first. "I made a promise to a little girl a few weeks back." He paused. "Our little girl. Will you help me keep it?"

She nodded. "Emmie knew all along that you'd be here. When I doubted, she knew."

"Then I'm a lucky man." He held out his good arm. "Shall we?"

When they arrived at the school parking lot, Maddox let Paige out close to the building, so she could catch Emmie and Logan before they went inside.

As she approached the crowd, a line of three high-beam construction lamps, positioned along one side of the gathering, lit the sidewalk for the arrival of the guests. Music played from a set of speakers on tripod mounts to the side, and a cordoned-off cluster of onlookers waved, hooted, and snapped pictures of each oddly matched couple waiting to enter.

As soon as she reached the crowd, Paige heard someone call her name. "Over here, honey!"

"Mrs. Mulligan?" Paige's eyes widened as the woman waved her over.

"Where's your date?" she asked as Paige made her way through the people between them. "Where's Maddox?"

"He's parking the car." Paige caught her breath. "And you—" she smiled "—are a tricky woman."

"Oh, I bank on forgiveness after the fact. My sweetheart can attest to that." She patted Hugh's arm next to her as he nodded and winked.

"Now, I think there may be one more surprise in the making. You go find that sweet daughter of yours. You'll want a bird's eye view for this."

Paige cut her eyes at Mrs. Mulligan. "What have you got up your sleeve now?"

"Just a little credit where credit's due. Go on, now, and enjoy the party, darlin'. She flourished her hand at the assembly of people in front of her. "This is all just adorable."

Paige hesitated, then turned and quickly shuffled back through the crowd toward the line where the children and their escorts stood.

Before she could reach them, the music faded, and Mrs. Forester, dressed now more ceremoniously than in her typical principal pantsuit, picked up the mic at the podium. Once the high-pitched squeal from the PA system evened out to accept her brassy voice, she began her greeting.

"Ladies and gentlemen, thank you for your patience. It is my honor tonight to welcome you to our annual

Father-Daughter/Mother-Son Winter Cotillion. We will begin in just a moment to announce all of our noted couples as they walk the red carpet and enter the building."

Paige continued to move shoulder to shoulder through the crowd. She finally saw Logan and Emmie, Ava and Toby close to the end of the line.

The principal continued, "Before we begin, however, we have a very special announcement." The crowd hushed as the principal paused. "Tonight, we would like to take a moment to honor one of our noted guests. Would Miss Emerson Westerfield's escort bring her to the carpet, please?"

Paige stopped, her eyes turning to the principal, then to Emmie and Logan shouldering through the crowd on the other side. She saw Carly and Jessie step from behind the cord, Jessie spreading her tripod while Carly kneeled on the carpet a few feet away, camera poised.

After Logan accompanied Emmie to the edge of the crowd and placed her in the center of the long red runner, he stepped back. Mrs. Forester continued. "Now, I'd like to tell you a quick story about Miss Emerson. She came to my office yesterday with her teacher to get an extra ticket for tonight's cotillion. You could understand my confusion when, on my list of guests, a ticket had already been reserved for her friend and escort, Mr. Logan Carter." Mrs. Forester nodded at Logan, who smiled and nodded back.

"Miss Emmie, however, insisted she must have one more ticket. Ladies and gentlemen, just this afternoon, I got a phone call informing me that Emmie's father was a returning soldier coming home from deployment as a Raider for the United States Marines."

"Mr. Carter"—she nodded to Logan—"we, of course, would like to extend to you a warm invitation to our cotillion as an honorary guest of Miss Emerson Westerfield; however, I think she may have acquired a new escort for the evening."

Logan acquiesced with a bow as Paige saw Maddox step into the crowd from the parking lot.

As if on cue, a patriotic score rose from the speakers in the background. "Ladies and gentlemen, please join with me in thanking Gunnery Sergeant Maddox Granger for his valiant service, and please show him a warm Camden Grove welcome home."

The crowd exploded with applause, whistles, and cheers as people moved to the side, opening a path for Maddox to the carpet. Paige could see the surprise in his eyes and his jaw tighten with emotion as they reached to shake his hand, offering him thanks, welcoming him home. Home to Camden Grove.

When he stepped to the edge of the carpet, Emmie broke into a run toward him.

Paige didn't hold back tears anymore. She couldn't. They came without reserve. She began to clap with the rest of the crowd as Emmie reached Maddox and threw her arms around him. He picked her up with his good arm and held her until she was ready to let go.

The long embrace inspired more applause and cheers even after Maddox kneeled, and Emmie stepped back to show him her open hand.

While no one else knew, Paige understood the significance of what she then placed in his palm. She knew it wasn't just a unique-looking lucky charm. The buckeye had become a symbol of a little girl's faith, her own proof that love, much more than luck, can bring someone home.

Maddox placed the buckeye back in Emmie's hand, enclosed his fingers over hers, then hugged her again.

Amid more applause, Maddox stood and scanned the crowd.

When he locked eyes with Paige, she weaved through clusters of people, crossed over the cordoned line, and met him and Emmie as they reached the edge of the carpet.

When they all three embraced, she paid little attention to the flashes of Carly's and Jessie's cameras. She didn't much hear the noise around her. The only thing she did notice was the Mulligans slip past the crowd and leave. Like that moment in the conservatory, Paige understood even more what it meant to find what she'd been looking for all along.

And the grandest miracle of all?

She didn't have to wait one second longer.

Epilogue

T he school gym, converted from the regulation-sized basketball court to the venue for a winter cotillion, now stood nearly vacant as the last of the guests wandered past the forest of borrowed Christmas trees to the propped-open exit doors.

Aside from Mrs. Forester and a handful of teachers, pacing from gym to storage room with tired decorations, a couple of school custodians swept up remaining cookie crumbs and waited for the last of the occupants to vacate before locking up.

Carly and Jessie were left to break down their backdrop and lighting equipment without interruption.

"Did you see the crowd's reaction when Maddox showed up? I think we may have just stumbled onto our next business experiment. Military homecomings. What do ya think?" Carly wound an extension cord around her arm from hand to elbow.

Scanning through thumbnails on her camera's display, Jessie wrinkled her nose. "Yeah, sure, if business ever slows down from our blind-date shoots, our engagement sessions, and wedding appointments. Oh, *and* if we move to a military base." She rotated her camera from portrait to landscape. "We did get some great shots. I even snapped one of Logan in the background, tearing up a little after Maddox scooped Emmie up into his one uninjured arm."

Carly smirked. "He's gonna love that."

Jessie set the camera on her lap. "I don't know about you, but I'm exhausted. And I still need to check on my mom."

"How's she doing with the new assisted living arrangement?"

"It's been a hard adjustment for all of us." Jessie unhitched the lens, capped it, and put it in the bag at her feet. "I think I'll make a trip to the car with this load." She gave a quick nod at the equipment on the floor. "When I get back, I'll help you roll up the backdrop."

"Why don't you go on? It'll take me only a few minutes to finish breaking down."

"Are you sure?"

"Of course." Carly closed the studio umbrella and set it beside the tripod.

"Well, I'll at least come in and grab another load." Jessie slipped on her jacket and put the heavier of her two camera bags over her shoulder. "I'll be right back." She then grabbed the light case and headed toward the front exit.

The night had been mentally exhausting as well as physically tiresome. She'd decided rather quickly that adults in blind-date, engagement, and wedding shoots made much easier photo subjects than elementary school kids and their parents, fussy for the perfect picture. She'd seen more tie straightening and spit-pasted hair in one night than she had the energy to recall.

Getting home to a nice warm bed and a good spy movie sounded like the perfect way to wrap up the day.

The temperature had dropped a few more degrees since they'd shot the outdoor candids a few hours earlier. Typical, Paige thought, for Alabama to have a December day warm enough for short sleeves and then a night that called for polar fleece.

As she stepped from the building, she pulled her hood on and cinched the jacket around her neck to block out the crisp air. She paid little attention to the utility truck a few spaces over.

Other than a vague awareness that some guy was loading the portable floodlights and that she'd parked entirely too far from the door, she gave little brainpower to anything except unloading the bag digging into her shoulder and getting back inside before the chill set in.

She later realized that paying little attention was her first mistake. When she stepped from the sidewalk to the bus lane, she hadn't even noticed the drop cord lying across her path.

When her foot caught the cord, the light case went flying in front of her, the camera bag came down with a thud beside her, and she landed in a face-plant on the pavement. All this just before a tripod supporting a mount of industrial lights came down in an impressive crash behind her.

Pain shot through Jessie's knee with the intensity of a knife stab. Her body drew up in a fetal curve, and her shriek echoed across the lot.

At first, she didn't hear the running footsteps behind her of the man approaching from the work truck. She was too busy trying not to cry out again, breathing in heavy gulps of air to push back the pain.

Then, his voice, just over her shoulder, added further insult to injury with a barrage of ridiculous questions. "Are you . . . are you alright, Miss?"

She couldn't speak at first for holding her breath. Then, in one caustic gush of embarrassment and fury, words rolled off her tongue in a verbal lashing that a spoiled child would have been hard-pressed to match.

"Whose stupid drop cord is that, anyway? And why would anybody be that careless?" She huddled over her knee, still rocking against the pain.

"I—I just took up the carpet. It was underneath. I was rolling up the cords, but you must've fallen over one."

The man circled her and kneeled in front of her. "Let me help you."

She huffed and blew as her entire leg began to throb. That's when she looked up from beneath her hood and first caught sight of the man kneeling to help her.

Her rocking stopped, and for a split second, the pain didn't register. But his eyes did. Even shadowed under a wrinkled brow, they pierced her—steel blue and troubled.

That's what she'd noticed about him the first time they met, not a month ago.

When she claimed he'd be the man she'd marry.

Dear Reader,

Thank you so much for spending time inside the pages of *Waiting for You!* Want to see more of Maddox and Paige's future, check out this **BONUS EPILOGUE** at **https://dl.bookfunnel.com/xyh0659hoi**

NEXT IN THE CAMDEN GROVE SERIES:
Holding Out Hope

Haunted by the heart-wrenching loss of his girlfriend six years ago, Dakota Renshaw shields himself from new love, fearing he might hurt others too. Destiny intervenes when he meets Jessie Galloway, who strives to break through his self-imposed isolation with friendship and hope. As Jessie battles to shatter his protective barriers, she wonders if her efforts will prove futile, leaving her entangled in her own kind of hopelessness.

Join Dakota and Jessie on an emotional journey in this poignant tale of healing, love, and the transformative power of hope. *Holding Out Hope*, Book 4 of the Camden Grove Series, will capture your heart and leave you breathless.

Check out my **WEBSITE** for this and other books in the Camden Grove Series, and sign up for my **NEWSLETTER** for release updates at **https://www.tessakinkade.com**!

Happy reading,
Tessa

Acknowledgements

Waiting has never been my strong suit. I am, however, grateful for those in my life who *have* waited, who *are* waiting, and who *will continue* to wait as I navigate this world of writing.

My editor, Jennia D'Lima, you have waited on my manuscript when I've been behind on a deadline. Your insights and suggestions improve my writing exponentially. Thank you.

My mentors in the writing community—KJ, Meg, Megan, Amanda—you have waited patiently on the other end of zoom calls, phone calls, messenger, and emails to answer questions I didn't even know how to formulate (and sometimes talked me off my ledges). I'm forever grateful.

My parents, you have likely waited for calls that should have come, for visits that may have been delayed, or for times that I wasn't present because a deadline was looming or an obligation hadn't been met. I hope you know what an inspiration you both are in my life, what impact you've had and continue to have in every decision I make, writing or otherwise. *Thank you* is too simple and inadequate.

My kids, you've waited on me while I've disappeared into my writing cave and, without complaint, welcomed me back with all the best hugs. I love you unconditionally.

My husband, the most patient of all. Waiting for me to brave the elements of the publishing world will be one of the biggest jewels in your crown. Thanks for asking long before I started this leg of our journey. How I love you!

My Father in Heaven continues to wait for me in all aspects of my life. How grateful I am for His constancy and love. I am His.

About the Author

As a child, Tessa Kinkade composed her first stories in chalk on her bedroom door. Editing was much more fun that way. Her workspace nowadays is still her bedroom, and she can often be found propped among her favorite bed pillows, tapping away on a laptop with a water bottle by her side (though she continues to look for easy ways to edit). Tessa has spent much of her career in education, and in her spare time—when her children were old enough to get their own cereal bowls from the cabinet—she began writing her first novel, 15 minutes at a time.

In the past, she's worked in a rape crisis center, kept bees, organized large events, run half marathons, and traveled most of the contiguous United States, drawing upon all her career experiences and hobbies to enrich her writing. She loves to create characters who face life-altering challenges yet find a happily-ever-after through the struggle.

When she's not bingeing on research, outlining, or drafting her next novel, you'll find her dreaming about a beach vacation where she might also find a lighthouse to explore.

Connect with Tessa for a free short story, information on new releases, exclusive extras, newsletter sign-up, and more at

https://www.tessakinkade.com

Also find her on social media:

https://instagram.com/tessakinkade

https://facebook.com/tessakinkade